Praise for *Expiration Dates*

"A passionate story about love and trust that will have you sniffling long before the twist."

—*People*

"This novel goes beyond a lighthearted romance to explore the ways we let fate shape our lives, for better or worse."

—*New York Post*

"Serle provides an interesting conceit and a healthy dose of wit that readers will appreciate. An entertaining love story with moments of depth."

—*Kirkus Reviews*

Praise for *One Italian Summer*

"A story about love, loss, and that point in adulthood where we learn our parents are human, too, and not always perfect."

—Associated Press

"Going down as easy as a limoncello on a hot summer's day, this day-dream of a story affirms what it means to love and be loved."

—*Library Journal*

Praise for *In Five Years*

"A profound tale of unconditional love and anguish with a touch of the mystical and mysterious."

—*New York Journal of Books*

"Serle's whimsical tale is book club catnip."

—*Publishers Weekly*

ALSO BY REBECCA SERLE

One Italian Summer

In Five Years

The Dinner List

YOUNG ADULT

Truly Madly Famously

Famous in Love

The Edge of Falling

When You Were Mine

Expiration Dates

A NOVEL

REBECCA SERLE

ATRIA PAPERBACK

NEW YORK AMSTERDAM/ANTWERP LONDON
TORONTO SYDNEY/MELBOURNE NEW DELHI

ATRIA
PAPERBACK

An Imprint of Simon & Schuster, LLC
1230 Avenue of the Americas
New York, NY 10020

This Atria Paperback edition October 2025

Interior design by Kyoko Watanabe

Manufactured in China

1 3 5 7 9 10 8 6 4 2

Library of Congress Control Number: 2023014903

ISBN 978-1-6682-0378-1

For J. Finally.

Tell the truth, tell the truth, tell the truth.

—ELIZABETH GILBERT

Chapter One

The paper is blank save for the name: *Jake.* The four letters rest on cream stationery lacking any additional information but sporting a firm black border. It's weighty, this note. Significant in my hands.

I find it slipped under my door on my way to dinner. The dinner that, if this paper is to be believed, will introduce me to the man I will spend the rest of my life with. This has never happened before. But then again, it's not the kind of thing that happens twice.

The restaurant is in West Hollywood, not far from where I live. I like to choose the place. If I get the paper late, like, say, at dessert—and it says two hours—I can wrap things up quickly.

Tonight we are at the tail end of summer in Los Angeles, and warmer nights are descending into the low seventies. The wind has even started to pick up—reminding us of all that fall can bring. I tuck my hair behind my ear and toss it over my shoulder as I climb the steps and open the door.

"Hey, Daphne!" The hostess at Gracias Madre, a casual vegan Mexican place on Melrose, recognizes me immediately. Her name is Marissa, and I know she used to bartend at The Pikey on Sunset, before they closed. "You're the first one here, do you want to sit?"

The space is beautiful—a bar area spills out onto a large and lively patio to the side. There are potted trees throughout the restaurant, and warm, yellow light falls from the overhead glass fixtures and onto the terra-cotta-tiled floors like honeycomb.

I'm nervous, and I'm never nervous. I'm wearing a black halter top and a pair of 501s. Neon kitten heels. I would have probably chosen a different ensemble, maybe even something a little more romantic, seeing as how this is going to be my last first date ever, but I was already dressed, and now here we are.

"Sure," I tell her. "I love your jumpsuit." I point to the denim romper she's wearing. I could never pull it off, but she definitely is.

"It's from the vintage on Melrose—I took your tip."

"Throwback," I say, as we walk. "Good shit."

There are several places in West Hollywood that sell second-hand, but Wasteland is the best. I don't have a ton of hobbies, but thrifting is one of the few.

She leaves me at the table—I'm in the back of the restaurant, which gives me a full view of the entire space—and I take out my phone.

There's a text from my mom, Debra. Honey, did you look at the pictures I sent? She's a burgeoning photographer, primarily focusing on—I kid you not—mezuzahs.

The answer is no.

One from my landlord, Mike, who wants to know if the

gardeners came today. I shoot him back an emoji. Also no. A flurry of pings on a group chat I have muted—college friends, something about Morgan's bachelorette. I haven't seen half of them in a decade, I'm surprised they're even including me.

And one from Hugo—my ex-boyfriend (we'll get there): Well?

He's not here yet, I write back. Then: Just sat.

I consider telling him about the fact that this time, for the first time, the paper was blank, but decide against it. *I'm about to meet my soul mate* feels like more of an in-person thing, or at least a phone call. We convey too many important things in too few words these days.

Drinks after? I'm meeting Natalie at Craig's, should be done by 8.

I try to remember who Natalie is. The girl he met at Bikram? Or the one from Bumble?

Maybe.

I put my phone facedown on the table.

Five minutes go by, then ten. I order a drink—one of their alt margaritas from the menu. Something with agave and smoked jalapeño. It arrives and goes down salty and tangy.

He runs late, I think. It's not ideal, but I can live with that. About five years ago, right around the time Hugo and I called it quits, I decided to start showing up to places on time. I've been pretty good about it. LA traffic notwithstanding. It's all about learning the rhythms of your city. Don't try and get to WeHo from Brentwood in the afternoon. There is always construction on Wilshire by Westwood Boulevard; take Sunset. San Vicente to Seventh Street to the Pacific Coast Highway is the slowest way to get to Malibu, but the most beautiful.

My phone dings. Another text from my mom: ?

My parents live in the Palisades, on the other side of the 405 in Los Angeles. The Palisades is like Pleasantville—all the new houses belong on Cape Cod, and there's a shopping center that takes holidays a little too seriously. It's also about as far as you can get and still live in the same city.

Love it! I write back, without opening her email. Last week she sent me an entire Dropbox full of her rabbi in various states of undress in the backyard. I consider explaining to her that just because she loves Judaism and photography does not mean all her photography has to be Jewish-influenced, or that her Jewish identity now has to be caught up in being a photographer, but I decide against it. It would take more than two texts, and I want to be present right now.

Present.

Thirty-three years, six significant relationships, forty-two first dates, one long weekend in Paris.

And now, here we are. The first and last blank sheet of paper.

"Daphne?"

I look up to see a man not a lot taller than I am, with graying brown hair and hazel-green eyes. He's wearing a button-down shirt and jeans and carries a single red rose.

"Hi," I say. I make a move to stand up to—what? Hug him? I sit back down.

He hands me the rose. When he speaks his voice is pleasant and familiar. "Someone was selling them outside, and I thought I should bring a proper consolation for being fifteen minutes late."

When he smiles, the lines around his eyes crinkle.

"You were right," I say. I take the rose. "What took you so long?"

He shakes his head, like, *Oh boy*. "How much time do we have?" Jake asks me.

I take him in. Real, incarnate, across from me now. He has a birthmark under his jaw, a freckle by his left eye. All of these minute details that make up a person, that make up this person, my person.

"A lot," I tell him. "We have a lot of time."

Chapter Two

It started in the fifth grade with a postcard. I had just come home from soccer practice and found it waiting on my desk in my room, right on top of my dog-eared copy of *Jessica Darling*.

Seth, eight days. The postcard was of Pasadena—bright lights, big city. *Huh.*

I showed it to my parents. "What is this?" I remember asking them.

They didn't know. They were busy, then, in those earlier days. My mother worked for a Jewish nonprofit, and my father was head of West Coast sales for a new water-filtration system. The company would fold five years later, and my father would go into pharmaceuticals for a few years before retiring entirely. My parents had always been relatively frugal, and the ups and downs of their financial life did not seem to affect them the way they did most people. At least not to me. We were comfortable. I didn't realize until much later that my parents had made a lot of deliberate choices to live within their means in a town that encourages keeping up. We had the smallest house on the best street so that I could go to a great public school. All that mattered to my mom was that she had space for a garden—her roses are legendary, and in Southern California they bloom on a rolling schedule from March straight through October.

"Who is Seth?" my father asked. He was by the stove, sautéing onions. My father has always been an equal participant in the kitchen and on the cleaning committee. When my grandparents, his parents, first immigrated to this country, my grandfather opened a kosher deli. Everyone was needed and had to learn to work both behind the counter and sink—including my father.

I thought about it. Seth. I knew who he was. At least, I knew who *a* Seth was. He was a grade older than me at Brentwood School. He also played soccer, and we were often on the field at the same time. Sometimes after practice if there was an extra blue Gatorade he'd give it to me. I didn't like blue Gatorade—as far as I could tell it was the one to be avoided, because it turned your mouth an unsightly shade of purple—but I liked them from Seth.

"A kid at soccer?"

My father turned, pointed the spoon at me. "Start there."

The next day after practice, there was no blue Gatorade. I made the first move.

"Hey, Seth."

He was tall, with blue eyes and about as many freckles as dots on a ladybug. Red hair, too.

"Hi."

"Did you send this to me?" I shoved the Pasadena postcard at him.

He laughed. "No," he said. "That's funny."

"Why?"

He looked genuinely perplexed. "I don't know. It's a postcard."

I cannot express how we went from this riveting exchange to him being my first boyfriend, but that is what happened. He asked if I'd like to accompany him to the Bigg Chill, and then we dated for one week and one day. The breakup was mutual. We were better off as friends.

And from that point on, that's how it happened. Sometimes it would be a postcard, sometimes it would be a sheet of paper, once it was a fortune tucked into a cookie. Sometimes the note would come after I'd met him, or right before, or in the case of Hugo, six weeks in. But it always told me the same thing: the exact amount of time we'd spend together.

Up until this evening, that is, when it gave me no indication of an end at all.

"How is the margarita?" Jake asks me. "I'm more of a vodka guy."

Vodka. Interesting. "Good," I tell him. I cock my head to the side. "Spicy."

Jake laughs. "Are you trying to make me uncomfortable? Kendra told me you do that sometimes."

"No," I say. "Am I?"

He looks at me. "A little bit, yes." He clears his throat. He seems to straighten an invisible tie. "But it's not bad."

Jake and I were introduced through my colleague Kendra. Or my ex-colleague. I work for a famous producer, someone you've never heard of who has made every movie you have. Irina is her name. Kendra was the old me.

"I think you should meet my friend Jake. He's thirty-five, newly single—but not in a rebound way—and works in entertainment," Kendra told me over lunch at the Grove. The outdoor shopping mall in Los Angeles looks like a Hallmark set twelve months a year. There's a Santa train at Christmas, a giant bunny at Easter, and a *Gilmore Girls* gazebo the whole year through. There are always twinkle lights and a fountain that's flow is set to Sinatra songs. What started as a joke—"Want to have lunch at the Grove?"—had quickly become tradition. We both loved the Cheesecake Factory.

"Actor?" I asked.

"Television exec."

"Boring."

"Stable," Kendra said. She lifted a fry into her mouth. "Nice-looking, too."

"That means unattractive."

"No, it doesn't. Nice-looking could mean hot."

"It could mean cute; I'm willing to give you that much. It definitely doesn't mean hot."

"You don't want to marry someone hot, anyway."

I figured if it was meant to be, time would soon tell.

"Sure," I said. "OK. Set it up."

It's not that I do not want to get married or even that I do not want to get serious with someone, it's just that it's not up to me. Something else has always called the shots in my life—call it the universe, fate, the comedic force of timing. But my life isn't like other people's. I have a different set of rules to live by.

Jake orders a margarita, too, and we get chips and guacamole for the table; the "crab" cakes, made with hearts of palm; an order of mushroom fajitas; and a rice bowl that comes with an overwhelming amount of cilantro that does not appear to be destemmed.

"You think we should get the grapefruit ceviche?" Jake asks.

"Let's skip it," I say. "Grapefruit's not my thing."

Once Marcus the waiter leaves, Jake takes out a notebook.

"I'm sorry," he says. "I have this weird thing I do where I have to write down every time I see someone wearing Doc Martens."

"You're kidding."

Jake shakes his head, bent over the notebook. "I'm not. It started in college as a kind of joke and then just continued."

"Any kind of Doc Martens?"

Jake looks up at me, stone-serious. "It has to be the black boots."

I spit out my margarita. Some combination of lime juice and tequila flies out of my mouth and toward his face. I can see the drops fly—slow-motion molecules. My eyes go wide. I put a hand over my mouth.

"I am so sorry."

He wipes some liquid from under his eye with his pointer finger. "I deserved it. It is admittedly a very strange thing to do."

I hand him a paper napkin from the table. "I like strange," I say.

He takes the napkin and dabs at his face. "Oh, thank God, because tucking in my tail gets very uncomfortable after an hour or so."

"You're funny," I say. "Genuinely, I'm having a good time."

Jake balls the napkin and then he closes the notebook and tucks it back into his pocket. "Excellent," he says. "Same here."

We discover over the course of dinner that we are both fans of

Shakespeare, that we love green apples but not Fujis, and that we are both night owls.

"Too many activities value early risers," Jake says. "Jobs, gyms, farmers markets. Even hikers in LA judge you if you get there past nine."

I lift my drink. "Hear! Hear!"

"There should be an evening farmers market for people like us where the latest arrivals get the best things."

"I like the way you think."

"I'm glad." He smiles. "So what's your job like?"

Jake's on his second margarita, and his cheeks are a bit flushed. It's endearing. It's been a while since I encountered a man who couldn't hold his booze.

My job is a little bit of everything. It is chaotic, sometimes toxic, fun, infuriating, and most importantly, flexible. Which is exactly how I'd describe my boss, too.

"Irina is a little nuts," I say. "But I like her. Or, I get her, maybe, is a better way to put it."

"Kendra told me she once made her go through trail mix and pick out only the peanuts? Why not just buy peanuts?"

I shrug. "She likes the overall trail mix flavor. You can't argue that they don't taste different."

"You pick out her peanuts?"

I laugh. "No way," I say. "Kendra still comes over for that."

To be honest, none of it seemed that crazy to me. Over the course of the past three years, Irina and I had developed a rhythm. I knew how she took her coffee from every chain on the planet (oat milk misto at Starbucks, oat flat white at Coffee Bean, black coffee with steamed oat milk from Peet's), that all of her groceries should be organic but if they weren't, she wouldn't actually care. That she liked to use miles to upgrade but if you couldn't guarantee an upgrade, you should book first class. That you could schedule meetings for the morning but they'd never go well, and that every hotel she stayed in had to have a gym. In exchange she didn't question if I needed Friday off, or came into work at eleven on a Monday.

We had the unicorn of all relationships in Hollywood: a functional female-female one, with a power dynamic at play, to boot.

"She's just particular," I say. "But aren't we all?"

Jake seems to give this more consideration than I feel is necessary. "I don't think I'm that particular," he says finally.

"Really."

"You're judging me."

I pick up a corn chip and spoon some salsa on top. "I'm not."

"You are," he says. "You're doing that thing with your eyebrows."

"What thing?"

"There's a thing," he says. He points to the space right above the center of his eyebrows, and wiggles them.

I snort out a laugh, and some salsa gets stuck. I take a big gulp of water.

"I am judging you," I say once I've swallowed.

"I know," he tells me. "But I don't mind as much as you'd think."

"Why's that?"

He puts his elbows right on the table and leans forward. "I think you're going to let me get to know you."

I think about the blank piece of paper in my bag.

"You never told me why you were so late."

"My car broke down," he says.

"That's it? That's not even a real thing."

"Cars breaking down? I can assure you it happens all the time."

"Like a flat tire?"

"Like the carburetor."

"I don't know what that is."

All of a sudden Jake looks uncomfortable, and I wonder if I'm pushing it, treading somewhere I shouldn't. The car is clearly an excuse. There is a familiarity I feel, with the information I have, that maybe isn't appropriate yet. This is only a first date.

I've had to watch that in the past. I know what someone will mean to me before they do, before I should. Who cares about his car anyway?

"It doesn't matter," I say. "At least you drive. I feel like everyone in LA Ubers now. I like the idea, but it makes me too carsick."

Jake smiles lightly. "You could sit up front."

"I'm not a big fan of small talk."

"Me either," he says. "But then I end up being rude and talking on my phone in the back seat."

"I find that hard to believe."

As soon as I say it, my cell phone starts to vibrate on the table. I slip it off and flip it into my bag, but I can see Hugo is calling. Is it nine already? Two hours have gone by quickly.

"I'll get the check," Jake says.

"No worries," I tell him. "It's my best friend. He's just calling to see how tonight went."

Jake responds as he flags down a waiter. "What are you going to tell him?"

I wait until he's turned back to me to answer. "Solid prospect. Has a shoe fetish. Worth further evaluation."

He blinks at me slowly, and I feel something unhook in me, like a necklace falling. For such a comfortable night, it's not such a comfortable feeling.

"I'm glad Kendra set us up," he says. "I don't meet a lot of women who seem to have the sense of self you do."

"I feel like that's a compliment to me but an insult to my gender."

"Not at all," Jake says. He is so sincere it's almost shocking. "I just don't meet a lot of women."

I choke back a laugh as the waiter hands us the check. Jake reaches into his back pocket and pulls out a card. I make a move to take out my wallet, and Jake puts a hand over mine, stopping me.

"Please," he says. "My treat."

I think about making a joke, usually I would. Something about the exchange of my company. But instead I thank him.

Jake walks me to my car—a 2012 silver Audi I affectionately call Sullivan. I got him off an actress who had a long-running Fox sitcom and then promptly moved back to Canada when it was canceled.

I notice walking next to him that Jake is a bit taller than I thought earlier. Or maybe it's just his presence. There is a certain warmth to him that makes him feel larger or more pervasive. In the way he pulls back my chair, in how he holds the door open, in the way he places his hand, gently, on the small of my back when we cross the street in front of a waiting car.

We make it to my meter. The night is stunning around us—clear and warm and crisp, all at once.

"This is me," I say. "And this is Sullivan."

Jake considers the car. "Can I call her Sully?"

"Him," I correct.

Jake holds his hands up. "I don't like to make assumptions."

Then he lifts one hand up to cup my elbow. "Can I see you again?" he asks.

I nod. "I'd like that."

He doesn't hesitate—he leans down and kisses my cheek. His lips are soft, but then again, most lips are.

"Drive safe," he says.

"No broken carburetors here."

He rolls his eyes. "All right, good night."

I watch him check the street both ways and then jog across, up the block, before I get inside. I open my bag. Sure enough, there are two missed calls from Hugo, and a text: Must b good. I'm at Laurel. U coming?

And then I take out the paper. It occurs to me that I should not have stuffed it down into my bag. I should preserve its integrity. It is, after all, the final note. The one I have been waiting for. It shouldn't be bent or crinkled.

Luckily, it's held up well. Just some granola crumbs. I brush them off.

Jake, it reads. No more, no less.

Just finished, I write. Give me twenty.

I want to tell someone, and he's the only one I can. Daphne Bell has finally met her match.

Chapter Three

Hugo, three months.

We met in an acting class, or outside an acting class, rather. Neither one of us was there to act. I was picking up a young actor who had recently been hired for a new show on the network that employed me as an assistant. We were due back on the Warner Bros. Studio lot in fifteen minutes, and the class was running over. At this rate, if we left now, we'd be ten minutes late.

I was standing by the doors to the studio in Hollywood, hopping from foot to foot and checking my watch, when a guy who looked like he was auditioning for the James Dean reboot showed up beside me.

"You're late," I told him. "The class is almost over."

He had arrived in a convertible Porsche. It was parked haphazardly next to Sullivan.

"I'm picking someone up," he said. "I'm not an actor."

I laughed. Because honestly? I'd never seen someone who

looked more like one. And my life at the time consisted of mainlining audition tapes most of my waking hours.

He kept watching me. "I'm trying not to be insulted," he said.

"You're wearing a white shirt and a leather jacket."

He looked down at his torso, considered it. "You should have seen what I had on before this."

I noticed his stature, how tall he was. I'm not a short woman, five foot seven without a slouch, but he was towering. Hold-your-head-back-in-your-hand-and-look-up kind of tall.

"How about yourself?"

"Also not an actor."

"That part I got," he said. He smiled at me. He had some serious dimples. "Seeing as how you seem to have disdain for the profession."

"I never said that."

His eyes flitted briefly from the ground and back up to me. "You didn't have to. I'm Hugo, by the way." He stuck out his hand.

"Daphne."

His fingers were long and cool. He had a silver ring around his pointer.

Then all at once the doors burst open and out walked the class.

My actor, Dionte, led the pack. A twenty-two-year-old kid with a smile that made me feel vaguely Mrs. Robinson–esque. "We're late, I know. He wouldn't let us leave before scene study."

Dionte pivoted my elbow and started leading me back to the car. But not before I saw a slender brunette slip herself into Hugo's arms.

Obviously, I thought.

I ran into him again five weeks later. By that point I had

become somewhat of a fixture on the Speiser/Sturges circuit. Dionte didn't drive—his father had died in a motorcycle accident when he was just twelve years old, and it put him off being behind the wheel. So every Tuesday and Thursday I'd pick him up after class and bring him back to set.

It was now early June, and the weather in LA was turning from jeans and a T-shirt to tank top, shorts, and a water bottle.

When I arrived in the parking lot, Hugo was already there. This time he was wearing a white-and-blue button-down and a pair of loafers. He looked like Clooney.

I wasn't sure he'd recognize me, but as soon as I stepped out of my car, he waved.

"Daphne, hi."

"Hugo, right?"

He smiled wide. "Still not an actor. Although I did take up talk to text, briefly, if that counts." He held up his hand. "Carpal tunnel."

"The modern injury." I hooked my bag over my shoulder and took some steps toward the door.

"Who are you here for?"

"An actor."

He looked amused.

"I have to pick him up for work. I'm an assistant at CBS. He's on a new one-hour drama."

Hugo nodded. I didn't ask his motivations; they seemed obvious.

"Do you like it?"

"Picking him up?"

Hugo coughed out a laugh. "No, the show."

"Haven't seen it."

Once again the doors opened. Dionte walked out, similarly concerned about the time. I let him get into the car and made my way back slowly. I was just opening the door when I saw a girl fling her arms around Hugo's neck. She was not the same girl from five weeks ago. This girl had blond hair. And a belly ring.

"Are we late?" Dionte asked from the passenger seat.

"Yes, but the great news is you can just blame me," I told him. "That's what I'm here for. Your call-time shield."

The following Tuesday Hugo's Porsche was parked neatly in a spot, and Hugo was sitting on the hood. Jeans, black polo, one foot planted on the tire, the other dangling toward the ground.

"Are you just doing a round-robin of the whole class?" I asked.

"Hello," he said. He looked genuinely happy to see me, but also that's how his face was. Always animated—you could read how fast his mind worked by how emotive his face got. "What are you getting at?"

"That actresses in this class seem to be your type."

He looked to the door and then back to me. "Maybe I'm just the type of the actresses in this class."

"That line is a rip-off." I locked my car behind me.

"Jack Nicholson," he said. "I know."

Annoyingly, I felt my stomach pinch. He knew Nancy Meyers.

"I'm starting to feel like we're parents in the carpool lane," I said.

"First off, I really wish you wouldn't cast me in a paternal role here. Secondly, I'm not here to pick up anyone today. In fact, I need to jet before class lets out. Cassandra really fucking hates me now."

"You're kidding," I deadpanned.

"You're funny."

"So why are you here?"

Hugo unhooked his foot from the tire and stood. "To see you, obviously."

I snorted. Hugo's eyes went wide.

"No way."

Hugo nodded. "Way."

He was attractive. Tall, dark, handsome. Well-dressed, clearly successful. But he was also arrogant, that much was as obvious as the cologne that wafted over to me in waves. And arrogance tended to devolve into unkindness quickly. I wasn't interested.

Plus, there was no paper. No name, no amount of time.

"I'm flattered, maybe, but I'm not your type," I said.

"Why's that?"

"Just trust me on this one."

"Oh, I do, but I'm curious."

Dionte came outside. He was alone. "Scene study is running over, but Tracy said I could leave." He looked at Hugo. "Hey, man."

"Hey."

"I didn't want to make them wait. Julie hates it when I'm late." Dionte pivoted toward Sullivan.

Hugo came over to open the door for me. I stepped inside, and he closed it using the window.

"I think you're fun. And sexy," he said, leaning down. I felt myself blush but ignored it. "Can you just give me your phone number?" He dangled his cell phone back and forth through the window.

I glanced at Dionte in the passenger seat, busying himself with a script, pretending not to hear what he clearly could.

"I'm not like other people," I told him.

Hugo narrowed his eyes at me. "I know."

I started the car. Hugo backed away from the door.

"Hey," he said. "Hang on. Shit. Looks like you got a ticket." He plucked the paper off my windshield and handed it to me.

I opened it, using my body to shield the words. *Hugo, three months.*

I couldn't tell if I was relieved or angry. The last relationship I'd had was four years earlier—for six months—and I'd been handed long weekends ever since.

But here we were. At the start of ninety days.

I pointed to his phone.

"Hand it over," I said.

Chapter Four

Hugo is tucked up into his corner courtyard table when I get there. I duck into Laurel Hardware off Santa Monica Boulevard, waving to the hostess and descending the stairs to their back patio. It's a beautiful space—tables scattered throughout and lights strung up from overhead trees. Casual, fun, and the food is epic. "Lollipop" Brussels sprouts, duck fried rice, and the best pan-seared salmon I've ever had.

I expect to see Natalie next to him, but instead there are three guys at the table, one of whom I recognize as the manager of this very place.

"You're here," Hugo says. "Amazing."

He leans up and kisses me on the cheek. "Daph, this is Sergio and Irwin; you know Paul—" He cocks his head at the manager; I give him a half-wave. "And, guys, this is Daphne."

I take a seat. Hugo hands me a tequila soda. My after-hours drink of choice. Now Hugo drinks them, too.

"We're taking off," Irwin says. "But look, Hugo, if you talk to Alexandra and she agrees, then we'd consider it."

Hugo nods. "I really think it's a great opportunity, guys."

"Just let us know," Sergio says. He turns to me. "Pleasure."

"You too."

They depart, and Paul goes back to work.

"Are those the guys talking about 820 Sunset?"

"Yep. They stayed another night to tour the space today. I canceled dinner with Natalie. She wants to fucking kill me."

"What's new?"

Hugo shoots me a look. "Don't start. It's been a day."

"I thought that sounded like good news." I point to the guys, to where they've just gone inside.

"Alexandra is never going to agree. She thinks commercial real estate is dead, and they know that. They're playing me."

Alexandra is Hugo's business partner. I've met her a few times. She's an ex–naval officer turned finance wizard, and somehow has time for three kids, to boot. From what I understand about Hugo's job, he convinces very rich men (like Sergio and Irwin) to invest in very expensive buildings in the hopes that real estate is always on the up. 820 Sunset is their new prize.

"So," he says. "How was it?"

I take a sip of my drink; it's strong. I'm not a lightweight, though. I had two margaritas at dinner and just feel pleasantly buzzy.

"Different," I say.

Hugo leans back and puts an arm over the empty chair next to him. "What does *that* mean?"

"Hugo," I say. "The paper was blank."

Hugo is the only one who knows about this love-life oddity, this strange anomaly in the cosmic universe of which I am the recipient and participant.

"Bullshit."

"I'm serious." I can feel my heartbeat in my ears. I haven't let myself think about what this means, not really, not entirely. Not yet.

I see Hugo's face react. Surprise to confusion to something else that I do not wish to identify. "Wow."

"Yeah," I say. "Wow. He seems great. His name is a Jake. He's a television executive for Warner Brothers."

"Of course he is." Hugo thinks anyone who works in entertainment is "low speed." *It's an industry full of people who are semi-available eleven to four and think they're brokering world peace.*

"Hey," I say. I point my finger at him. "Be cool."

"What do you think this means?"

I shrug. "Only one thing it can mean, right?"

Hugo nods. "I sort of thought if it would happen it would say, like, forty years."

I swallow down some more tequila. "I guess no second marriages here."

"Blank space," he says. "Like forever?"

I clear my throat. "Or until time runs out. Dependent on how you look at it."

"How uplifting." Hugo leans forward. He holds up his glass. He's drinking Scotch or whiskey—I never know the difference. "Daph, do you like him? Like, is he who you imagined for yourself?"

I consider the question. I didn't realize there was a pattern to the notes until well into high school. After the third one it became clear—what they meant, what they were telling me. I looked back and thought, *Huh*, and then, *Oh*. But I still wanted forever love. I still wanted my perfect mate, my smiling husband. I'd picture the white tulle dress and the lace veil and a man who was kind and attractive and who my parents loved, because why not.

But as time went on, the fantasy got stale. I tried to update it, keep it fresh. Sometimes we eloped to the cliffs of Capri. Sometimes we went to Vegas and I wore a tight white minidress. And the man evolved from being kind of amorphous to being specific, detailed. Mariah Carey and Frank Sinatra replaced Disney tunes, and then we rounded the corner into Van Morrison. What can I say? I wanted a love story that *sung*.

Sitting here with Hugo now, talking about Jake, I can't help but feel like he's a little bit of a throwback, that he belongs to a Daphne who didn't quite understand her life yet. Or who maybe believed more was possible than any thirty-three-year-old woman has any right to.

"He's really nice," I say.

Hugo snorts. "He's *nice.*"

"Nice is underrated."

"You're probably right." He sets down his drink. "Well, look, I'm happy for you. When do I get to meet him?"

"We should go on a second date first."

"You mean before you break the news to him that he's your soul mate and also your best friend looks like this?" Hugo gestures a hand down his torso.

"Right, something like that."

His cell on the table rings. "It's her."

"Pick up."

He does. "Hey, babe, how are you?"

I can hear her through the phone. I can't make out her words, but the tone is clear—she's not happy.

"I know, listen. Hey. Hey." His voice gets soft. "I'm sorry. Listen. Genuinely, I am." He turns away from me and cups the receiver, even though it makes no difference, I can hear every word. "I'll make it up to you, I promise." He pauses. "Yes. I know, babe. I do. OK. OK, bye." He hangs up.

"That went well."

Hugo shakes his head and downs the rest of his drink. "I don't know. Work is so strenuous and chaotic lately. I feel like I don't have time to breathe."

"You like it that way."

Hugo looks across at me. "Do I?"

"I'm sorry, are you intimating you'd rather be at home with Natalie right now than trying to charm Tweedledum and Tweedledee into a two-hundred-million-dollar building?"

Hugo grins. "You're right."

I hold my glass up to him. "To your future," I say.

"And to yours. Looking bright."

I think about Jake. About the kiss on the cheek.

"Bright or radioactive?"

Hugo considers this. "A lifetime with you could only be one thing."

Chapter Five

On our first date Hugo took me to the Tower Bar, a well-known restaurant in a well-known hotel on Sunset Boulevard. The hotel is old-school and infamous—the cozy scene of late-night celebrity diners and traveling *Vogue* editor meetings. Irina is a frequent guest. Dimitri Dimitrov was the maître d' for over a decade—there were articles published about his retirement in 2018. He knew every customer's name, favorite table, drink order. I remember thinking Hugo had to be one of his regulars.

We sat at a table outside, right at the edge of the pool. The courtyard is beautiful, with overhead lights, and on many Saturdays, a band that plays jazz, Sinatra, and Bing Crosby.

"Romantic," I told him when we sat down. It was almost eight, and the sun was nearly fully set, the glamour of the place coming alive in the burgeoning darkness.

"This is one of my favorite spots," Hugo told me. "I've been coming here for a decade; it never gets old. When people say LA isn't magical like New York, I take them here."

I considered Hugo's age, then. I tended to date men who were my age or younger—I liked their carefree spirits, the way they didn't have a fully molded mate in their mind you were constantly trying to live up to, but Hugo was at least five years older. Seven, actually, it turned out. I knew I was not the kind of woman he normally dated, and it made me feel insecure—or more generously, on edge.

"It's beautiful." Across the pool was the Los Angeles skyline, a floating city in the clouds. Palm trees and towers and homes, side by side. That's the beauty of LA—it's sprawling, searching, a horizontal buffet of experiences. In New York, everything is happening on top of everything else—energy and expectation, stacked up like dominoes. Here, you have to hunt for what comes next.

Something always happened to me once I got the paper—I became resigned. I knew what was coming. I felt, sometimes, like I'd hacked the system. Wasn't the hardest part of heartbreak the unpredictability? How you could feel the most connected to a person in one moment—like being in a teardrop together, the world a watercolor outside—and like strangers in the next? Friends were always talking about how they did not see it coming. But I did. There was no need to dive in headfirst only to realize the proverbial pool was empty. I knew when to invest, and for how long. And when the end came it was sometimes painful, often disappointing. But I could never say I was blindsided. I could never say I didn't know.

Hugo was wearing a black Henley and dark jeans. He had on a leather necklace around which hung a pendant I would later learn was a key to the first building he'd ever bought—a small two-story on Pico that was now a restaraunt. "It's a family-run place, and Pico was their first expansion, their second location."

Hugo was proud of his work, it was obvious. He talked about it with rapture—almost like a child who can't quite believe his luck.

A twentysomething waiter came over.

"Calvin, what's up?" Hugo said.

"Not much, man, how you been?"

"Good, good." Hugo smiled in my direction. "This is Daphne."

Calvin gave me a little bow. "Pleasure."

"Hi."

"You guys want something to drink?"

Hugo held his hand out to me. "Ladies first."

"A tequila soda," I said. "With a lime, if you have."

"You got it."

Hugo nodded his approval. "Scotch for me, whatever you're pouring."

Calvin left, and Hugo turned back to me. "Calvin had a bad accident a few years back. Some asshole on Mulholland. He couldn't work for about three months, and he ended up crashing with me for a few weeks."

"At your apartment?"

"House," Hugo said.

I saw him note my surprise.

"I'm not there that much."

I studied him. "So, what? You're a do-gooder?"

"Gotta offset the karma somehow." Then he shook his head. "Nah, he's a good guy."

What I remember from that dinner is that Hugo seemed

sincere. Which was surprising, and made me feel a little foolish—like I, too, was falling for it. Like I couldn't tell the difference between an act and the real thing. I had felt so different in the parking lot, but maybe I was the same. Maybe all it took was a fancy restaurant and a story about being someone's savior.

"How's it going with the kid?" Hugo asked.

"Dionte? Good. They don't really tell me much, though. I'm on a need-to-know basis. He seems to like the class."

"Cassandra did, too."

"What about the brunette?"

Hugo smiled at me. "You think I'm a foregone conclusion."

I swallowed down some tequila. "I know you are."

He leaned forward. "Is that a challenge?"

"I don't think it can be," I said. "I don't think you want the prize."

Hugo sat back in his chair dramatically, as if I'd socked him. He didn't immediately say anything. A moment passed. I let it.

"I do, though," he said finally. "At least, I think I do."

Three months was enough time to figure it out and not get stuck underwater. I'd had only two bad breakups before, and I couldn't even say they were bad—they were just painful. Most of them ended cordially, if not friendly. It's hard to have a falling-out when one person isn't outraged. The paper made it so that nothing was personal. When Ben Hutchinson cheated on me during sophomore year of college, I wasn't even mad at him. Of course he had, it had already been four and a half months.

"Those are two very different statements," I said.

He looked at me. When he spoke, it felt like a confession. "I know."

We ordered—steak for me and grilled salmon for him. Another round of drinks, french fries, and sautéed spinach. Hugo ate with careful bites, slicing off small bits of salmon and spinach, laying them on the back of his fork with care.

"How do you consume all of that?" Hugo asked me, gesturing to my plate. "You're thin."

"Good metabolism," I said. Conversations around weight bored me. There were so many more interesting things to talk about than the particular shape of someone's body.

Hugo could sense that he'd lost me.

"Can I just say I find you very enjoyable?" he said after a moment.

I picked up a fry, dunked it into the ketchup. "I'm flattered."

"I don't think you are," he said. "But regardless, it's true, I do."

I uncrossed and recrossed my feet at the ankles. "Thank you." What I felt was: *Uh-oh.*

When I was twenty-four I briefly lived in San Francisco. I moved for an internship with an app that went belly-up six months after I got there. San Francisco was a weird city—all the conformity of DC with the lush, green hills of a freethinking Pacific Northwest. And still in California!

I met a man there named Noah who was getting a doctorate in meteorology. I knew from our first date that he was going to be trouble, and when the paper came it said: *five weeks*. I remember thinking: *That's too long.*

By which I meant: *It isn't enough time.*

He was from Texas, with a slow drawl and just the right amount of facial hair and blue eyes that when he looked at you felt like they were missiles. Noah showed me the Golden Gate at sunrise and the Haight in September and the best Indian place in the whole damn city. When five weeks were up, I didn't want it to end, but then he got the call: a grant in Iceland. That was a Friday. He left the following Tuesday.

I can't say I was surprised. There are some experiences you just have to have.

When Hugo and I were finished with dinner, Hugo got up from the table and went over to the guitarist.

I watched him negotiate, slide a bill into the man's hand, and return to our table. I gave him a questioning look; he just shrugged.

And then a song began to play. The first dangling notes of "Ribbons in the Sky" by Stevie Wonder: "'*Oh, so long for this night I prayed that a star would guide you my way . . .*'"

Hugo was looking at the guitarist intently. And then his gaze turned to me. "Too much?"

I wanted to say, *Yes, of course, ridiculous* [eye roll]. *Who does this work on?*

But instead I shook my head.

"I'd ask you to dance, but that seems embarrassing."

"Try me."

Hugo pushed back his chair and stood up, offering me his hand. I took it.

I was wearing a black dress, fitted at the top, flowy to the ankles. He placed his hand right along the seam of my back.

From the corner of my eye I saw people at neighboring tables watching us. I felt an unfamiliar sense of anticipation, the stirrings of something unexpected.

"I like the way you smell," Hugo said.

I liked the way he smelled, too. The cologne had transformed. I wanted to bury my nose in the crook of his neck.

His fingers played down my back.

"What do you think?" he whispered. "Should we give it a whirl?"

I pulled back to look at him. His face was lit up in a smile.

"OK," I said. "Why not?"

He lifted my arm, and spun me.

Chapter Six

I drop Hugo at his house—a Spanish-style three-bedroom on a rose-lined street called Ashcroft smack in the middle of West Hollywood and Beverly Hills. By the time we leave, it's been over an hour since I've had anything to drink, and I feel dead sober, the reality of tonight sits upright like another passenger.

Hugo lives about eight minutes from me, but his house is in another world. It's classic, charming, with just a hint of history—and perfectly maintained. Bright green moss grows over one exterior wall and ivy on the other. The greenery offsets the big, glass windows.

"Do you want to come in for a drink?" he asks.

"School night," I say. All of a sudden I feel exhausted. "And I have to get back to Murph."

Hugo's car sits in the driveway, underneath an ivy-covered archway. There's a bike parked to the side, Hugo's helmet dangles from the handlebars. Evidence of a life, however pristine, in motion.

But there is something strange about Hugo's house I've never exactly been able to put my finger on. It's beautiful, and inside, impeccably decorated—it has much more personality than I ever expected it to have the first time I came here. I remember thinking I'd find lots of glass and chrome, but instead I was met with oversize velvet chairs, textured antique fabrics, and a blue-painted kitchen. It looked warm and welcoming, but it still gave me the feeling of emptiness somehow. Like if I opened any given drawer in the kitchen I'd be met with blank space. Once, when Hugo was in the shower, I went to his bookshelf and cracked the spine of a copy of *Underland* by Robert Macfarlane, just to make sure the pages weren't blank. Not only were they not blank, but they were etched with blue ink—Hugo's notes and markings.

"I picked out none of it," Hugo once told me, but as time went on I became less and less convinced that was true. Now, I know it isn't. Hugo loves aesthetics. I've been with him to the Saks on Wilshire to pick out new suits. He has a personal shopper at Brioni, a tailor who calls him with the latest Prada styles. The man likes to look good, and he likes everything around him to look good, too.

Hugo leans across the front seat and gives me a quick hug. "Later, babe. And happy for you."

"Thanks. I'll talk to you tomorrow."

I watch him close the car door and walk up the front steps. The sensor picks up movement, and the lights flick on, illuminating his wood-and-brass door, the white stucco of the house.

I wave and back away.

It takes me seven minutes to drive home, but by the time I get in, it's twelve minutes past midnight. My dog, Murphy, doesn't bother to get up when I come in, just moves a little to let me know his sleep has been disturbed. I took him for a walk earlier, so he'll be good until the morning.

I got Murphy for my twenty-sixth birthday at Bark n' Bitches on Fairfax, a place that has sadly since closed. He's a terrier mix but there's something else in there, too. He's bigger than most terriers, with a softer coat.

Murphy was never interested in anything canine. It is my genuine belief that he is a 1940s banker who was once cursed by a witch to live in a dog's body. He sniffs almost nothing and is appalled by the game of fetch. *You want me to catch a ball? With my mouth*? I imagine him saying. *How uncivilized.*

"Hi, buddy," I say. I go over and scratch his ears. He gives me a cordial nod before going back to sleep. I kick off my heels and stretch my toes onto the wood floor. It's cold underneath me—Los Angeles buildings have absolutely no insulation, and it's freezing at night, especially in the winter months. I really need a carpet. And a space heater, maybe.

I live in a small apartment building on North Gardner two blocks off Sunset. There are five units and a shared courtyard between them. Each apartment has its own entrance—mine just happens to be street-facing.

The apartment is big—bigger than it should be for what I'm paying. Mike hasn't raised my rent in nearly four years, which is unheard of in this part of town. There's an open living room, a roomy kitchen—although the marble is dated, and the cabinets are peeling—and a back bedroom with a walk-in closet. When I first moved in, I painted the hallway and living room in a sage green. The place is decorated haphazardly—in prints, neutrals, wood, linen, some vintage orange Bakelite lamps I picked up at the Rose Bowl Flea Market. And curtains from Pottery Barn. I have too much stuff.

I drop down onto the couch. I know I should just stay in motion—teeth, pajamas, bed. Keep going until I can lie down. But even the bathroom feels too far right now. I tuck my freezing feet underneath me.

On my coffee table is a copy of *For the Love of Shakespeare*, a gift from Irina that was representative of an inside joke I now can't quite remember. I love it unironically, though.

"Her passions are made of nothing but the finest part of pure love."

Here's the truth: I do want love. In some ways, I've been looking for it forever. Real love, the kind that makes you want to grow old together, makes you not just unafraid of all that time with one person but electrified by it.

I assumed at some point, maybe, the papers would stop. But I wasn't looking forward to that day, at least not exactly. There was something in me that wanted to keep moving. If you never stop long enough to sink into something, then it can't destroy you. It's easier to climb out of a pool than a well, is the thing.

None of this is particularly unique, or revelatory. We live in an age of romance where you can pick from thousands of strangers on the internet. Pretty much everyone fears buyer's remorse. And yet—

I hoist myself off the couch, driven by dehydration, and pour a glass of cloudy tap water from the sink. You're supposed to drink only filtered in Los Angeles, but I stopped refilling my Brita about a week after I purchased it. There is no way that thing was clearing out anything, anyway. The only change I could see was the addition of black dots to the container—which did not seem like much of an improvement.

I do miss the thing I don't have. It's strange to feel that, to want something that you've never even known before. But that's love, isn't it? The belief in something you cannot see or touch or even explain. Like the heart itself, we just know it's there.

I walk over to the back door and look out over the courtyard. It's empty and silent. Overhead, the sky is heavy with midnight clouds.

I wonder if I'll miss it, I think. The feeling of openness. The understanding, even buried down deep, that anything could happen. That I could bump into someone at an airport or in line at the pharmacy. That the man three stools over at the bar could be taking me home tonight. That the next great adventure was just a slip of paper away.

Being single is like playing the lottery. Most of the time all you're left with from that trip to the convenience store is a bag of chips and a six-pack. But then there's always the chance. There's always the chance, however slim, that with one piece of paper you could win it all.

Chapter Seven

Martin, three days.

I was racing down the steps to catch the metro and already late for set in the first arrondissement—a full thirty-minute commute from the portion of Paris I had been stashed away in. I'd been there for three weeks, assisting on a shoot for my brand-new boss, Irina. I had replaced Kendra just ten days before we'd left for France, and now I was playing catch-up, halfway around the world.

"What are your thoughts on living in a foreign country for a month at very short notice?" Irina had asked me in our interview.

I looked at her razor-sharp black hair, perfect cigarette pants with crisp creases down the middle, and starched white button-down, collar slightly popped. If this artfully constructed woman could be spontaneous, so could I.

"They are excellent," I'd told her. I thought about Murph, but he loved my parents, so I knew it would be OK.

And now, here we were.

"Excusez-moi! Excusez-moi!" I stopped short to see a fifty-something woman with a manicured bob pointing to a letter on the floor. God, French women really did know how to pull it together.

"C'est le tien!" she continued.

I picked up the envelope. Inside was a note: *Martin, three days.*

Normally I'd be intrigued. Three days in a foreign country sounded like a prospect, but unfortunately, I was still late, and I had no idea who Martin was.

I slid into the metro car just as the doors shut. Because the film was on a tight budget (films are always on tight budgets, even when those budgets are two hundred million dollars) they'd put me up in the sixteenth arrondissement, far away from where the rest of the cast and important crew members were staying. I didn't mind. I'd never been to Paris before, and I've always been a quick study with maps. I've had a sense of direction since the second grade—call it my perennial need to get out of the Palisades. My father helped me turn it into an adventure, and as he drove me to a beach past Point Dume, or a new ice cream shop, I would unfurl the map onto my lap and just stare at all of Los Angeles laid out before me.

I got off the metro at the Tuileries/Pyramides stop and raced across the street. Today we were filming by the Ritz Paris, in the Place Vendôme right in front of the storied hotel with the same name. Iconic. Every time I looked around at the smooth gray stone and the chic French people and listened to the beautiful whispered language, I couldn't believe my luck. Here I was on a movie set in the city that was already the most famous movie set in the world.

The movie was a remake of *Paris When It Sizzles*, a 1964 film starring Audrey Hepburn. The studio had wanted to use a hologram of Audrey, but Irina had convinced them it would be better with a real-life starlet: "You need someone for the publicity tour. What are you going to do, project smoke in a room and have *Variety* fire away with their questions?" But as it so often goes, the starlet wasn't living up to Audrey's ghost. If they'd have asked me (which, of course, no one did), I'd have said, "Le duh."

I made my way rapidly down Rue de Rivoli, and ducked into the Starbucks six streets over. Everyone on set wanted coffee, and everyone wanted Starbucks. Paris is a city that despises Americans but loves American chains. I think Parisians secretly like all the choices—oat milk with cinnamon and stevia? Perfect.

I made it to the front of the line and handed over my list. One of the assistants typed it out in French, and I brought it with me daily. Before we developed this system it took me half an hour to order.

As the cashier rung me up, I used the time to check my phone. There were two texts from Irina inquiring about my whereabouts, and one from Marguerite, the director's assistant, asking if I could add a triple espresso to the order. I flagged down the barista and made it happen.

By the time I got to set Irina was annoyed. She tended to sit when she was relaxed and stand when she wanted to throw something at you, I had learned. When I got there, she was pacing.

"Finally," she said. She made a *Gimme* motion with her hands, and I handed her the oat milk misto from the stack.

Marguerite, a pale French girl who did not look a day over eighteen but was actually thirty-one, took the rest out of my hands and distributed them accordingly.

"What time is it?" Irina asked me.

I flipped over my phone to read the display. "Eight thirty-five."

"And what time was call?"

I stared at her; it seemed redundant to answer.

"I'm sorry," I said. "I'll start leaving earlier."

I could see her appraising me and her demeanor shifting from punishing to empathetic.

"All right," she said. "Go get yourself a glass of water, or something. I don't like seeing you flushed; it's unsightly."

I deposited my own coffee in the empty chair behind her and made my way to "crafty," a few long tables where all the snacks and food for the day are stationed. Because we were shooting outside, they had erected a small tent to cover the area, about fifty feet over from village, or command central—where all the bigwigs, including Irina and the director, watched the scenes for the day. Irina had arranged for me to have a chair as well, and whenever they set up hers they set up mine, right behind her.

Craft service in America is mostly traditional snacks—granola bars, fruit platters, popcorn and chip bags. Dependent on the budget, there are extensive lunch and dinner spreads—salads and sandwiches, but basic stuff. In France it's an entirely different enterprise altogether. On our first day shooting, lunch was poached salmon, a fresh green and herb salad, baguettes, an eight-cheese spread, and crème brûlée for dessert.

All French films have wine at craft services, but American productions don't allow it.

I found a room-temperature water bottle above a cooler and downed it appreciatively.

When I looked up, I saw the actor who was playing William Holden's character, the love interest of the Audrey Hepburn role, at the coffee station.

He nodded to me; I nodded back. His name was Jacques, a French actor who had done a Marvel movie eighteen months ago and was now looking for some upmarket clout.

And then there was his stand-in.

Every time a new scene needed to be blocked or lit, this man would become Jacques, while Jacques went to change or to hair and makeup or to argue loudly in his trailer with his Brazilian husband, Lucas.

The stand-in looked like Jacques from the side and the back, but from the front he was rounder, and his features more prominent, less organized. He also had a thick beard. His name, of course, was Martin.

I decided to let the whole thing play out. Usually when I got the paper, I felt engaged, called to action—an immediate co-conspirator. I'd been deployed. I had a role. This time I wanted to see what would happen if I did nothing—if, perhaps, I appeared even mildly antagonistic. I can't say I was particularly attracted to Martin. He didn't speak too much, but then again, he was also a stand-in.

The day passed with little ceremony. The scenes in the courtyard were beautiful. The exteriors of Paris remain unchanged over the years—there seem to be more building codes and regulations than anywhere else in the world—creating a calming, unified effect. Gray and beige stone mounted together to form a city of cool neutrality. I'd never seen anything so organized look so beautiful.

Contrasted against the gray palette, Lily, the movie's lead, wore a fuchsia suit. Cinched at the waist with a hat to match, the ensemble was supposed to be a nod to the iconic lime-green suit Audrey once wore in *Paris When It Sizzles*, the original. The remake, incidentally, was just to be called: *When It Sizzles.*

Lily looked stunning.

Jacques appeared in a slim-cut Prada jacket with a fuchsia pocket square. Watching the two of them saunter through the courtyard was like seeing the first bold swipe of red paint hit a white canvas.

Art, I thought. I'd never seen it so alive before.

The sun was descending by the time we wrapped for the day, which meant it was after nine. In the summer in France it could be light until nearly 10:00 p.m.—the city bathed itself in every pastel color before bed. A slow ritual of yellow to pink to violet to baby blue. The joke on set was that the easiest job in French cinema is the lighting department.

I saw Marguerite carrying some boxes over to a waiting car.

"Is there anything else you need?" I asked Irina. I pointed to Marguerite, who was clearly struggling. "Otherwise I think I'm going to help her."

Irina looked over. "I don't want you lifting those," she said. She studied me. "Suppose you hurt yourself and can't make it tomorrow?"

I glanced back at Marguerite. Martin had stepped in, they were now loading the boxes together.

"See?" Irina said. "Get a man to do it. That way, they can be good for something."

We talked about the schedule for the next day, and then I said good night and hooked my backpack over my shoulders, preparing to make my way to the metro. The evening was warm, and I didn't mind the walk, but calculating how many transfers (three) I'd need to make before finally getting to my door sounded a bit insufferable.

"You need a ride?"

Martin pulled up next to me on a Vespa. I thought he was French, but when I heard him speak, he didn't have an accent. He was American, just like me.

I considered the weight of my backpack, and the many, many metro steps.

"Please," I told him, and got on.

Chapter Eight

Martin took me to a café close to my apartment, for crepes and fries and cold glasses of beer.

I learned that he had gone to the Sorbonne for acting and had stayed in Paris on a work visa. He was twenty-five, four years younger than me. When he spoke, there was a familiar warmth to him, a lumberjack transported to the streets of Paris.

"What do you want to do?" he asked me. We were a few rounds in already.

"I just started working for Irina," I said. "So this, for now." The truth is, when it came to my career, I felt a little like a feather in the wind. It wasn't that I wasn't ambitious—I worked hard; I was reliable and resourceful. I didn't mind long hours or menial labor. I liked to be busy. But I wasn't sure in what direction that energy should be focused. I felt like I kept sidestepping, instead of leveling up. I'd been an assistant in three different industries now, and in Hollywood, two different roles. I felt like I should be climbing toward something, or at the very least, climbing. But I loved the job, what little I knew of it. I loved how industrious I had to be, moment to moment. I liked that it required me to be nimble and present.

"I was an assistant at a network before, and it was too corporate for me. My boss was cool, but I didn't totally jive with the politics of an office."

"There are plenty of politics on a set," Martin said. "It's crazy. Even village has a seating chart. There's a hierarchy to who can order coffee!"

"Speaking as the person who has to pick it up," I said, "I appreciate that."

Martin took a swig of beer. We let the moment stretch.

"I guess I like being where the action is," I said. "And I'm not super concerned with what my job is within that. I know I'm the lowest rung, but who cares? I get to be here." I gestured around—to the lively café, the laughing couples, the cigarette smoke, the checkerboard-print tablecloths. To the smell and heartbeat of this foreign, familiar city.

He took another sip. "That's a fair answer."

"How long have you been in Paris?"

"Almost six years," he said. "There was a period after I graduated where I had to leave every three months, but now it's a lot easier."

"Did you get married or something?"

He smiles at me. "Actually, yes. To my best friend, Fiora. We don't live together, and we're not together; she has a girlfriend, but the French authorities seem to think that is perfectly reasonable."

"Yes, I heard that about the French."

"Does that freak you out?"

Up until then, I realized, there hadn't been a particularly romantic vibe. Because of the paper, I assumed there was, but in fact, had I not known, I'd have thought we were two coworkers out for friendly after-hours drinks.

"I don't know why it should," I said.

Martin nodded. "Have you ever been to Paris before?"

I shook my head. "I've never even been to Europe before."

He chuckled. "How much do you value sleep?" he asked.

"Pennies on the dollar."

"Excellent answer."

Over the course of one weekend, Martin took me everywhere. All the obvious places—the top of the Eiffel Tower and Notre-Dame, and Montparnasse to eat at a café and watch what all those artists in the 1920s found so inspiring. We explored the Gothic cathedral of Basilica Saint-Denis, and walked along the Seine until the sole of my sneaker gave up and detached from my shoe.

"I'll carry you," Martin told me, slinging me onto his back. We made it a minute before flagging down a cab while laughing hysterically at my flapping footwear.

The sex was not awe-inspiring, but it did not need to be. It was good, and I was happy to have it, happy to have this experience, skin on skin, in this city of all cities.

I had, in the past, often found sex to be dissociative, like I became someone else, or just departed the premises when my clothes came off. It wasn't that I didn't enjoy it, it was that I enjoyed myself enjoying it more. It was like I was watching myself from a distance—the sexy part was the fact that it was happening—sex!

In Paris!—not always the actual physical act, the sensation, the hum and thump of two human bodies. I liked the narrative, the story I was going to tell—was already telling—about what was happening.

Afterward we shared a cigarette on his balcony. Martin lived on the fringes of the seventeenth, with views of Montmartre. I was wearing his shirt—blue, emblazed with DODGERS in white.

"Do you ever miss America?" I asked him.

He stopped and inhaled. He was wearing sweatpants and a plain white Hanes T-shirt. I wondered if he'd purchased a single clothing item in the last six years, or if everything he owned in Paris was a hand-me-down from another life.

"Sometimes," he said. "Like if I want to go to a diner on a Sunday or just watch football or something. Maybe sometimes I miss how efficient things are in the US. Like how doors work both ways."

I gave him a look.

"It's ridiculous to have a set of doors that only go inward and a set of doors that only go outward," he said. He demonstrated with his hands. "I do not know why it's the standard here."

"That's it?"

Martin exhaled. I smelled the smoke. It felt fresh and new and heady.

"No, I miss a lot. But none of it is going anywhere. I'll be back someday, and the doors will still go both ways."

He smiled. I didn't say anything, and he continued.

"I hope I find someone like you there when I do. You make everything feel good, Daphne. Really good."

He walked toward me and put his hands around my waist.

He leaned down, and I kissed him softly, then felt his head settle on my shoulder. I looked at his studio, the mess of sheets, our Indian takeout containers—red and green curry, mango chutney, a brochure from Musée d'Orsay. How much had occurred in just three days' time.

"I'll miss you," I said, and meant it.

I felt his homesickness—or was it mine—pulsing through both of us like a heartbeat, and I knew I would miss that, too. The particular feeling of being twentysomething and lost in Paris, together.

Chapter Nine

Jake calls me the next day. Murphy is sitting upright by the coffee table, looking at the muted television as if he's willing the station to change. Fair enough, *House Hunters* is on.

The phone rings at three o'clock, right in the middle of the day.

"Hey," he says when I answer. "How are you?"

"I'm good," I say. "I'm at work."

It's only partially true. I'm at home, but I'm going over a budget for Irina's next shoot. She's producing a foreign commercial, which she does occasionally as a cash grab. It's a low lift, but she'll want this back by the end of the day.

"Right, of course, sorry about that. I'll make it quick."

"Not at all. I'm happy to hear from you."

I mean it, too. His voice is warm through the phone.

"Excellent. Listen, the reason I'm calling is that I have tickets to this comedy show tonight. It's outside, in Hollywood. It'll be one of those things—whoever is in town comes and does a set.

You never know exactly who will be there. There's a rumor tonight that Seinfeld may show."

I feel myself smile. "Really?"

"Do you want to come with me?"

"Yes," I say. "Definitely." I tentatively have plans with Kendra to go to dinner, but she'll be thrilled. Number one, I'm seeing Jake again. Number two, about two-thirds of the time she cancels our plans, anyway.

"I can pick you up," Jake says. "If you'd like. Or we can meet there, whatever you prefer."

"Let's drive together," I say. "It will give me a chance to assess your road skills."

He laughs. It's hearty. "All right, then. Shoot me a text with your address, and I'll pick you up at seven. Cool?"

"Cool," I say.

He shows up at 6:55.

He knocks twice in rapid succession on the door. I'm still one leg out of a pair of jeans, swiping on my mascara. Murphy doesn't bother moving from the bed.

"Just a second!" I call.

Why is he early? Everyone knows you're supposed to show up on time to a restaurant and late to someone's house. I can feel the quick-fire drill under my chest. I take a moment to steady my breathing.

I button my jeans, yank on my cropped orange sweater, and pad to the door without shoes.

Jake is standing outside, wearing jeans and a navy-blue sweater.

His hands are tucked behind his back and he's wearing glasses—a new addition. He looks handsome, and older than he did at Gracias Madre. More weatherworn, maybe. In any event, it's attractive.

"Hi," I say.

"Hi," he says. He pulls open the door farther. "You look lovely."

"Thank you. Here, sorry, come on in."

I hold the door open, and Jake steps around me. I let it swing shut behind us with a clang, a cool burst of air follows it.

"Just give me a second," I say. "I'm almost ready."

Jake looks around the place. It's tidy—I cleaned up a bit before in anticipation, but the amount of things I've accumulated over the years of living here make it hard for the place to appear completely orderly. There is just too much stuff for the space.

"I like it," Jake says, unprompted. "It feels like you live here."

I laugh. "That I do."

I go into the bedroom and locate my shoes—brown leather platforms. The thing about LA is that it can feel like summer up until December. But tonight appears to be an oddly crisp evening. They're closed-toe.

"Can I get you anything?" I call back to him.

"I'm good," he says. "We should probably get going, when you're ready."

I throw a lip gloss, a credit card, and an ID into my clutch, walk back to the living room, snatch my keys off the counter, and gesture for him to follow me out.

We walk to his car. It's a black BMW that does not appear to have a single scratch on it.

"She looks like she's back in tip-top shape," I say.

He smiles. "I left Marigold at home."

"Marigold?"

"Unlike you, I'm a feminist. My cars are women." He smiles at me. "I have a vintage Chevy, she breaks down a lot."

"Ah."

Jake opens the passenger door for me, and I slide inside. The car smells like pine cones, and I look up at the center mirror to see an air freshener tree hanging. I flick it with my finger as he settles into the driver's seat.

"I genuinely didn't know they made these anymore."

"Hey now," he says. "I'm a Pacific Northwest boy. I like to bring a little of the forest with me wherever I go."

"Portland?" I ask.

"Seattle," he says.

"I've never been," I tell him. "All I know is what I saw in *Fifty Shades of Grey*."

He looks at me dead-on. "The most accurate representation of our city I can think of. Great work."

Jake starts the car, and we drive up to Sunset, and then over to Hollywood Boulevard.

Hollywood is, in my opinion, the worst part of Los Angeles. Each side of the street is lined with star plaques, it's normally crammed with tourists, and is home to such iconic locations as the Madame Tussauds exhibit and the Hard Rock Cafe. Tonight there are droves of teenagers, and a few families in matching oversize T-shirts that have things like STEWART FAMILY VACATION printed on them. A couple poses for a photo, crouching to the ground, pointing at a star, the name of which I can't make out. Dolly Parton is a major attraction. I say that to Jake now.

"Do you know she has two stars on the Walk of Fame?" he says. "Not many people do."

"I did not," I say. "All I know is that Hollywood is the Times Square of LA."

"True," he says. "Although I don't know a ton about New York. I've been only a handful of times, and the last few trips I never left Brooklyn."

"I like Brooklyn," I say. "I wanted to live there, but I just never made it."

"We can't do it all, right?" He changes lanes. "How was growing up here?"

I consider the question. Some people tend to think growing up in Los Angeles is like growing up in Hawaii—or a constant episode of *90210*. Days spent shopping the palm-tree-lined streets of Beverly Hills, nights spent around bonfires at the beach. In truth, there were both of those things, but when you live here, Beverly Hills is just the suburbs, and the beach is just the place you were least likely to get in trouble for drinking.

"My parents live in the Palisades," I say, gesturing with my hand behind us. "I went to school in Brentwood. It was normal, I guess. They worked hard to make it normal—my parents. But it was definitely still a town full of rich kids."

"Were you a rich kid?" Jake looks over his shoulder, then makes a left onto Fountain.

I can tell the question isn't leading, and he's not attached to a particular answer.

"No, not at all. I mean we didn't struggle. My parents could always pay our bills, as far as I knew. But we went on road trips for vacation, and I wasn't getting Prada bags if I got an A, if that's what you mean."

Jake smiles but doesn't say anything.

"Not that they would have done that even if they were loaded. They're not super fancy people; I guess it rubbed off on me."

"You're not a fancy person?"

"If I'm out of bodywash, I use dish soap in the shower."

"I don't think that's not fancy," Jake says. "I just think that means there is something seriously wrong with you."

He glances at me, and I lean back against the headrest.

"How about you?" I ask.

"My dad was an engineer. He worked for Amazon for a period of time, as well as a bunch of start-ups. He did pretty well, and he retired a few years ago, actually. And my mom has a shop in Madison Park. She sells pottery and jewelry and a line of CBD products that fly off the shelves."

"That's fun," I say. "How long has she had the place for?"

"Twenty years, at least. It's been through many different iterations. At one point in time, it was a grocery store."

Jake makes another left, and then we're pulling up to a parking lot. There is a line of cars to get in, and I crane around to see that the place is packed—girls in tight black jeans, tank tops, and beanies move in swarms. To the right, a man in a black T-shirt and cargo pants hands us a ticket and directs us to pull headfirst into a spot that looks like it could fit a motorcycle, maybe.

Miraculously Jake makes it.

"Alright, so," I say. "You're an excellent driver."

A comedy club has been set up in what appears to be a large alleyway between buildings. There is a stage in the center and tiered circular seating surrounding it. There are brick walls on two sides, and overhead is a white silk tent on which stars are being projected.

"This is actually really cool," I tell Jake. "I love it."

He smiles. "I know, right? I haven't been before, but my colleagues all went over the holidays and have been telling me since how amazing it is. It's cool to see what they've done with the space."

I'm reminded every time I go out somewhere I haven't been of how many hidden wonders there are in LA. How much unlikely culture is hiding just out of sight. Sometimes it feels like this town runs on billboards and Teslas, but, especially over the last decade, there is so much more diversity of business. Downtown is a haven of installation art and fusion food and, yeah, a layer of trash, too. It's real in a way Los Angeles never was, at least not in my lifetime—and New York used to be. And it's all here for the taking, if you just look.

We're seated at a two-top on the left-hand side of the room, and a waitress immediately comes over to take our drink order.

"Tequila soda," I say.

Jake nods. "Same for me."

"I thought you liked vodka."

"I do, but I don't really care what I drink. And I like trying new things. I'm just not that choosy. At least, not about alcohol."

I take a moment to survey the crowd. There is an older couple to our right—tourists, I intuit. The man keeps pointing up at the tented ceiling, and the woman leans into him, tugging on his T-shirt.

There is what can only be described as a bachelorette crew—loose, drunk, calling one another's names at an unnecessary loud volume.

I feel Jake touch my shoulder. "I think that's the owner," he says.

An attractive man in a graphic T-shirt and jeans circles a few tables to the left. He shakes someone's hand.

"This is an interesting scene," I say. "Are you into comedy?"

"Yes," he says. He says it definitively, almost adamantly.

"When I first moved here, the other assistants and I would go to the Comedy Store every Wednesday night, after work. We'd score pizza on someone's work Amex, and then head over in a caravan. You can buy tickets for twenty bucks, sometimes our bosses had them anyway, and we got to see incredible comedians."

I remember now that Seinfeld is rumored to be making an appearance here tonight. Given the fact that the place doesn't seem *packed* packed, that seems unlikely, if not still intriguing.

"All the greats," he continues. "Part of the fun of the scene in LA—and New York, too, I'd imagine—is that even the big-timers have to test out new material. So before they film specials or go on tour they're working the local clubs. If you come weekly you can see the jokes develop until they're hard-boiled."

When Jake gets animated, he talks with his hands. He gestures to me, to the stage, his palms opening and closing, his arms dancing.

"Do you work in comedy?" I ask.

"Ironically I'm in drama," he says. "Honestly, I got a job on someone's desk early on who was a big exec in the drama department at Netflix, and then it just sort of went from there. I like it, though. There is so much drama in comedy, and so much comedy in drama. I don't think the two universes are as separate as they used to be, unless you're talking about sitcoms. It's all blending together."

The waitress appears with our drinks.

"Oh, great," Jake says. "Thank you." He takes them out of her hands.

"Anything else I can get you?" she asks.

Jake looks to me.

"I think we're good," I say. "Thank you."

The mic glitches to life, and then I see a man onstage.

"Hi, everyone, welcome! Thank you for coming to our little corner of Hollywood. We have a great show for you tonight, as always. Some of the best of the best are here. We have a show every Saturday, and if you'd like to support our Wednesday night special, please go to the website. OK. First up I'd like you to welcome Vie Rosen!"

People start clapping and yelling.

I turn to Jake. "She's familiar."

"She's amazing," he says.

"Vie is a comedian, television host, and the winner of 2016's *Last Comic Standing*. She's filmed four Netflix specials and is about to go back on the road for her tour, 'Can Buy Me Love.' Please welcome Vie Rosen!"

Jake leans over and whispers in my ear. "I was at Netflix when she made her first special. I love her comedy."

Vie jogs onto the stage. I've seen her before. She hosted a show called *Bride Wars*. She was hysterical.

She's about five feet six, has a ponytail of wispy blond hair, and is wearing a white T-shirt with a black bra underneath. She looks cool. The kind of girl who declines a dinner of gossip for a second set on a Saturday night.

"Hello, everyone, welcome to your comedy tour de force tonight. Where are you all here from?"

Some people call out various cities, Vie has a bit for every single one. "Why are all fancy universities in small towns? The entire middle of the country is just filled with places where rich kids get shipped in to go to college and the kids who are from there stay and work at Walmart. Maybe if we invested a little more in education and a little less in the coke habits of lacrosse players we'd be better off."

Her comedy isn't centered around jokes, exactly—it's centered around revelation. For every laugh she gets, and she gets a lot, it's a laugh imbued with the natural comedy baked into the exposure of uncomfortable truths. The things we pass by and don't notice, or at least, don't call out. It's a comedy of relief, it turns out. It feels good to hear the things you think but don't say out loud. It feels good to just be spoken to honestly, for once. So much of our current moment seems to be pandering—she says that, too.

Vie does ten minutes, tops, and then exits the stage. I feel like I could watch her all night.

"I love her," I tell Jake.

He responds by slipping an arm over the back of my chair.

There is a twentysomething comic who goes by the name Trey Ire, who is also very good. My favorite part of his set is about LA traffic: "LA traffic is so bad. I once stayed in a relationship just so I could use the carpool lane." Then: "I mean, I can't turn left in Pasadena because someone changed lanes at LAX."

Next up there's a short guy I recognize as a character actor from the 2010s.

"Wasn't he in *CHiPs*?" I ask Jake.

He nods.

The guy is fine, but his comedy feels a little dated. I stifle a yawn. Jake notices.

"You want to duck out of here and get something to eat?" he asks me.

"Seinfeld?" I mouth.

Jake runs his tongue over his top teeth. "Yeah, about that," he says. "Seinfeld isn't coming."

"For sure?"

"Pretty certain," he says. He looks guilty, spits it out: "He was never going to."

His face is arranged into a tangle of emotions—I can see he's not sure how I'm going to take this and preparing for a variety of outcomes. It's also clear he is not a person who lies often, or well.

"You dangled Seinfeld to get me to go out with you?"

Jake nods. "I mean, there was a slight possibility, but honestly, it was slim to none."

"How do you even know I like Seinfeld?" I say. "Maybe it would have been a deterrent."

Jake stands, then offers me his hand. His palm is warm and calloused. "No way," he says, handing me my jacket. "Everyone loves Seinfeld."

Chapter Ten

Jake takes me to Pace in Laurel Canyon, a restaurant I have loved since I was a kid—my dad would take me here if we ever found ourselves on the east side. It's this Italian place that does a really solid dinner menu—but the main draw is the atmosphere. Midway up the canyon, Pace sits on the right side of the road, and in recent years the restaurant has taken over the parking lot and adjacent dry cleaner's. The best seats in the house are the ones by a heat lamp and glass window with a sign marked WASH AND FOLD.

"The canyon kind of reminds me of home sometimes," Jake says. "It's the only place in Los Angeles I can smell nature. Woodsy."

"Except when it burns."

"Right, then it just reminds me of hell."

The comment gives me whiplash coming out of Jake's mouth.

"Dark," I say.

"Sorry," he says. He looks it, too. "Just trying to keep up with your banter level. I think I missed the mark."

"You're genuine," I say. "I like it."

He smiles. I see his cheeks tinge pink.

We're eating—him, a red snapper. Me, a bowl of linguini.

"Do you go back home often?"

"I try to," he says. "It's not so far, but life gets busy. I wish my folks would come out more, but they don't love to travel."

"I get that," I say. My parents think Florida is leaving the country.

"We used to travel when I was younger—my sister and me and my folks. We went to Europe two summers in a row, and Costa Rica for the holidays one year. But as they've gotten older they've been less interested. My mom likes to garden, and my dad has his golf game." Jake shrugs. "They enjoy their routine."

"It sounds like they really enjoy each other's company," I say.

Jake takes a sip of his wine. "That too."

We never traveled much when I was a child. We'd go to Palm Springs for Christmas and Tahoe for the Fourth of July and that was pretty much it. My parents are liberal, sophisticated people, for the most part. You think they would have prioritized even Mexico, maybe, but travel was expensive, and it wasn't a part of what made our life distinct.

"How is your pasta?" Jake asks. He peers forward at my bowl.

"Good," I say. I look at him. "Do you want a bite?"

He nods. "Yes, please."

Jake is not a man who is afraid to say how he feels. To peer into a bowl of pasta and accept a bite.

I twirl some noodles onto my fork and then hold it out to him.

He doesn't hesitate, he puts his mouth around the fork and grabs hold of the linguine.

"Delicious," he says, red sauce on his lips.

I laugh and shake my head.

"What?"

"Nothing," I say. "You're just so honest."

Jake smiles. "I'm going to take that as a compliment."

His eyes graze my face—moving down to my lips and back up. I feel something come to life between us. The space that was once open, mild, if not inquisitive, is now kinetic and charged.

"Can I ask you something?" Jake says.

"That's a trick question."

He raises his eyebrows but doesn't say anything.

I take a sip of wine. "Yes," I say. "Of course. Ask away."

He looks at me. His eyes don't move off mine. "What are you looking for?"

I blink back at him. No man has ever asked me that before. At least, not a man who I was sitting across from on a second date. Other people have asked. Friends; friends of my parents; once, a local underground matchmaker. But never him.

"What everyone is looking for," I say.

"And what it that?"

I think about how to say it. Because *love* doesn't seem good enough, it isn't really what he's asking. He wants to know if I want something serious. He wants to know if I want to let someone in, all the way.

"To meet the right person, to be with someone I want to see in the morning and naked. To not be afraid to have a bad day around them. To be happy, I guess."

Jake nods slowly. I can't tell if he likes the answer. He does not seem disappointed or relieved.

"What are you looking for?" I ask, although I expect I know.

Jake holds my gaze. And then I can tell. I can tell he is about to tell me something that he doesn't want to. People always look a little sorry when they're about to say something that hurts. "I was married once," he says. "We were very young when we got together."

I don't react, just let him keep talking.

"We were high school sweethearts, and we got married pretty soon after we graduated college."

"In Seattle?"

Jake nods.

"Beatrice," he says. "But everyone called her Bea."

Something cold spreads across the back of my shoulder blades. I feel it circle around and flood my sternum.

"You didn't get divorced," I say.

Jake shakes his head. "We were just twenty-seven. It was an aggressive diagnosis. They gave her eighteen months, but she only made it a year."

I see tears fill his eyes. He's so vulnerable here. So open. My hands begin to tingle. I tuck them under me and cross my legs.

"I'm very sorry," I say. "That must have been devastating."

He swallows. He's not trying to hide his emotion, but he's not trying to have them boil over, either. I am familiar with this dance, the space between being open and being a liability. The fine art of dating.

"It was the hardest thing I've ever been through," he says. "Obviously. And I still miss her every day."

"I'm sorry," I say again. I'm not sure what's appropriate to say, or how to say what is. And I feel something else, too. Some withdrawal. I want to remove myself from what he has just shared. It's only our second date. Maybe this is too soon, too much. It feels private.

The thing no one ever wants to say about dating is this: It's hard to be real, sure. It's harder to let someone else be.

And then it's as if he can tell because I see him pivot, reorient himself. And for a brief moment I hate my inability to handle this. That I have failed to meet the moment, and now it is gone.

"You know what they say about a man with a dead wife?"

I brush myself off. "Great in bed?"

He laughs. It's genuine, full-bellied.

"Great for perspective." Jake takes my hand across the table. His fingers are warm even though the night is cool. I want to grab his hand and hold on. "I'm sorry if that's heavy."

"Life is heavy."

"Does it scare you?"

I consider the question. *No, yes.* "Should it?"

"I guess it depends," he says. "One thing I'm not so good at anymore is casual."

I think about the piece of paper. All that blank space. I think about Martin in Paris and Noah in San Francisco and Hugo in Los Angeles. I think about all the canceled plans and missed texts and miscommunications. I think about every time someone said *I just didn't think it was such a big deal.*

"So, serious," I say.

Jake shrugs. "I don't think the opposite of casual is serious, actually."

"What is it, then?"

Jake looks at me. His hazel eyes appear almost gold underneath the light of the heat lamp—tiny specs of sunlight. "Depth," he says. "The opposite of casual is deep."

Chapter Eleven

Stuart

Stuart and I met in high school. He was Mr. Advanced Placement—the kind of kid the teachers are scared of because when he challenged them, he was usually right. He had the highest IQ in our class (we took IQ tests, I guess, which seems kind of problematic, looking back). He also took the best notes; they were legendary. Color-coded, broken down by exam and cross-referenced with textbook page numbers. Rumor had it they were still in circulation. Naturally, Stuart was responsible for organizing the study rosters, if you were lucky enough to be in his classes.

I wasn't. I was more focused on getting kissed than getting into college. I'd been curious for a decade, and it still hadn't happened. Between the fifth grade and the eleventh I did not receive a single piece of paper. Stuart was also a senior, and we'd become fast friends. We were both on the debate team, and we were both frankly excellent at it.

My parents loved Stuart. He wasn't Jewish, but he was everything else. Smart, sophisticated, and headed to an Ivy League school. It wasn't romantic; we just had the same interests—mostly that we thought ourselves better than everyone else. We loved Russian novels, dinner parties, and pretending we knew anything about wine. It wasn't until seven years later, when I ran into him in New York City, that he became a prospect.

I was there visiting my old college roommate, Alisa, and we bumped into Stuart in line outside at Sadelle's one Saturday morning in May. Stuart looked great. No, better than that. He looked *famous.*

While in high school, he was pale, a bit doughy, with the kind of burgeoning intellectualism that borders on pedantic. Now, he looked like a banker who woke up at 4:00 a.m. to get in a workout before the market opened and had the number of the city's best florist on speed dial.

"Daphne, hi." He gave me a warm hug and immediately introduced me to his dining companion, a significantly older gentleman named Ted. "What are you doing here?"

I explained that I was in town to visit Alisa—she quickly introduced herself—for the weekend, and that I still lived in LA.

"I don't miss it at all," he said. "Can you believe it?"

I had temporarily moved back in with my parents. "I can, yes."

We ended up ordering and eating together, and when we were finished, Stuart asked if I had any interest in dinner that night.

"Only if you have the time," he said. "It would be great to catch up some more."

I noted how his T-shirt pulled against his chest when he moved. How he stood up every time Alisa or I left the table to use the restroom.

"That would be great," I said.

He picked me up at Alisa's at 8:00 p.m. She was living in the East Village at the time, in a third-floor walk-up she miraculously had all to herself. The dream of living in New York was one I had long resigned I would never have. Not because I couldn't see myself making it in New York, or because I didn't think I could figure out a way to be there on little money, but because it was clearly not the direction my life was moving in. As much as I longed to and would eventually put the 405 between me and my parents, I knew I didn't want half the country between us. I knew I couldn't tolerate that distance. I relied on them in ways I did not think a twenty-five-year-old should. But I wasn't sure how to get out of that, either. It would be another two years before I was assisting at the network, and it felt like all I'd done since college was float from one entry-level position to another.

But I still loved the city. The way things always felt like they were coming together. In Los Angeles things disperse, simmer, yawn. In New York they connect, spark, crash.

"You look amazing," Stuart said.

I had on black, wide-leg pants, and a lacy white top that hovered just above my naval. Strappy black heels I had borrowed from Alisa and long, dangly feathered earrings.

"Thank you," I said. "You too."

He wore a button-down shirt and dark jeans, and he looked as good if not better than he had that morning.

Stuart took me to ABC Kitchen, this big, airy restaurant in the Flatiron District. He ordered for us: flatbread and grilled carrots with cumin and butter radishes and a market salad, french fries, and halibut. One bottle of cabernet.

Not only was Stuart now accomplished—I found out he, predictably, worked for a bank and had just been made the youngest partner. But he also turned out to be as interesting as I always suspected he might become. He had recently completed a skydiving certification. He was on a list to go to the Republic of the Congo and hike with the gorillas. And in his spare time he had founded and sold a tutoring start-up that was now worth about twenty million dollars.

"How's it going in LA?" he asked me.

In high school Stuart and I had bonded over the fact that we felt we were special, different, better than the run-of-the-mill girls and guys at our school who ate frozen yogurt from the Bigg Chill and carried Louis Vuitton shoppers as if there were only one standard of belonging. But now, Stuart had made good on all of that potential. He had something to show for it. I wasn't sure what to say for myself.

"Figuring it out," I said. "After college I thought I'd maybe go to law school, but the LSAT was not my test."

"Yeah, the lawyer thing," Stuart said. "Not for me."

"Me either, apparently."

In truth, I feared my youthful bravado had stayed a little too long at the fair. It was past midnight and sloppy and directionless. It wasn't that I no longer had hopes and dreams for myself. At twenty-five there was a lot I wanted to accomplish, but I also felt stuck. I wasn't sure what steps I should take next, or in which direction. It felt like people at thirty were just waking up with fulfilling careers, but I was only five years away, and it didn't seem likely that was going to happen for me.

"Whatever you do, you're brilliant at. You always were. You had that magic touch that people just wanted to be around. You were cool. You started a table tennis league and got kids to stay after classes for it."

"Technically it was Ping-Pong."

"See?" Stuart said. "Cool. In high school I had the biggest crush on you."

I felt my body reactively flush. I had known that, of course I had. My parents had pointed it out, my classmates, even our Spanish teacher thought we spent way too much time together. But that wasn't how I saw him. Stuart was *the friend*, not *the guy*.

Years later, sitting across from him, I thought about how totally wrong I was.

"Come on," I said. "We were buds."

"Yeah, but I was still a teen boy. You were hot and smart, and you didn't give a shit."

"I did," I said. "I just faked it pretty well."

Stuart leaned toward me. He lightly threaded my index finger through two of his own. "And now?"

"Oh," I said. "Now I fake it *really* well."

Stuart's apartment hung over the East River. It was comprised almost entirely of windows. There was a gray couch, white matching chairs, and more stainless steel than I remember seeing in

American Psycho. But the view—the view was absolutely breathtaking.

He poured us each a glass of wine and then settled himself on the couch. "Come here," he said.

I did.

He put his arm around me. I leaned my head into his shoulder and then picked it back up again. He smelled like deodorant—masculine and clean.

"I've thought about you a lot over these years."

I pivoted to look at him. "You have?"

He nodded. "I always thought about reaching out, seeing what you were up to, but then life got in the way. Tonight sort of feels like kismet."

It had been a long time since I'd felt this desired. I felt powerful, heady, full on the longing of all these years. I remembered how smart he was, how intelligent and caring.

"I'll be in LA next month for work," Stuart said. "I'd love to see you again."

I looked up at him. His face was inviting me in.

"But I'm here now," I said.

Stuart leaned over me. He placed a palm flat against my cheek. "That," he said, "you are."

He kissed me—it was deep and good. A rooting kiss. The kind that lasts long enough that you start breathing through each other.

"I like you," he said. "I like you a lot."

"I like you, too," I said.

A fantasy started to sprout to life in my head. Stuart and I, finding each other all these years later. Me, the wild, untethered, still-searching girlfriend. Him, the consistent, successful, charming man. We'd host lavish dinner parties, now armed with all the knowledge we didn't have before. People would look at us and say: *Can you believe it? They met in high school.*

The sex was good. Stuart was skilled. He rolled me on top of him and placed big, open-mouthed kisses on my neck. I could feel myself fold to him, hand myself over in a way I had not in recent memory, maybe not ever.

His hands moved down my back, kneading and releasing the muscles in my shoulders.

He kept his mouth on my neck and moved one palm over my belly and held it between my legs. I felt myself press down, wanting friction, something to move against.

"Hey," he said, blowing the words into my ear. "We've got time."

And then slowly he began moving his fingers in circles. I exhaled out everything.

When it was over I went to use the bathroom in his button-down. I splashed some water on my face, noting how rosy my cheeks looked. It really is true what they say: an active sex life does wonders for your skin. I was due to head back to LA the following day, but I was already thinking about extending my trip. I didn't have anything particularly pressing to return home for, and I thought I'd stay a few extra days. We could get to know each other again. Fill in the gap of the last seven years.

I swished some of his toothpaste around in my mouth and padded back into the bedroom.

When I got there Stuart was sitting up, setting his alarm. I climbed back in next to him.

"Hey," he said. He kissed me lightly on the temple. "Listen, I have to get up super early tomorrow." He showed me the alarm clock, like proof. "Would you mind terribly if I called you in the morning?"

I looked down at my body—his shirt, hanging open. My bare bottom. I cinched it around me. "You mean, you want me to leave?"

"You're upset. Don't be upset. I just sleep like an animal, and I barely get four hours as it is."

"It's fine," I said.

I gathered my clothes up as he watched. I yanked my pants on and pulled the shirt over my head, turning my back so he wouldn't see my naked chest. I slid into the heels.

"Have you seen my earrings?" I asked him.

"Ah!" he said cheerfully. He plucked them off his nightstand, handing them to me.

I reached to take them, and he pulled his hand away, using the other to grab my waist and drag me down into a kiss.

"This was a lot of fun," he said. "I'm really glad I bumped into you."

I strung the earrings through my ears. I felt all at once like a Christmas tree on December twenty-sixth.

"Yeah," I said. "It was fun."

He walked me to the door. He kissed me goodbye. There was no more talk of a trip to Los Angeles. There was no more talk of anything at all.

Outside, the night had turned cool. I hugged my arms to my

chest and started walking west, away from the water. After about a block I noticed something stuck to the bottom of my shoe. I teetered on the street, using my right hand to peel the paper off.

Stuart, one night.

I dropped the paper into my bag, and kept walking.

Chapter Twelve

On Sundays Hugo and I go to the farmers market at Melrose Place—a small outdoor market with six produce stands, the good bagels, and excellent sundried-tomato-infused feta cheese. It's also near Alfred, a coffee shop that makes the world's best iced latte.

In addition to the food, the market has the most gorgeous bouquets of roses—purples and pinks and deep burgundies. And giant, heady sunflowers to take home, too. There's also a clothing stand with patchwork coats in the winter and Coachella-inspired cover-ups in the summer. I love it here. I'd love it even more if Hugo didn't make us go before 10:00 a.m.

Hugo wakes up and runs six miles every morning, and his route spits him out right by my apartment. He ends up coming over around nine, when I'm just emerging, and we walk over together, Murphy trotting at my heels. It's become somewhat of our weekend ritual, if we're both in town, which I always am and he seldom is.

At 9:03 he texts me from the sidewalk: Where r u?

I pull on a sweatshirt and stick my head out the door. He's in a moisture-wicking black T-shirt and shorts. He has an armband around his bicep where he keeps his iPhone, but right now he's texting on it.

"I need two minutes," I mouth to him.

He pops out an earbud. "Yo," he says. "Good morning."

"Do you want to come in?"

Hugo shakes his head. "No, I want you to come out."

I close the door without responding and slide my feet into my favorite pair of burnt-orange Birkenstocks. I grab my wallet and an I ♥ NY tote bag from off the counter and leave with my keys.

I meet him back on the sidewalk. Murphy stays home. I showed him his leash and he didn't even pick his head up.

"You look like you had fun last night," he says when I'm outside.

"I do?" I'm wearing bike shorts and an oversize sweatshirt.

Hugo eyes me. "Well, I mean, you look tired."

"Wow, what a compliment." I slide my tote bag over my shoulder, and then Hugo loops it off me and carries it down by his side.

After dinner at Pace Jake dropped me back off. He didn't kiss me. I thought he was going to, but he leaned in, kissed my cheek again, just like last time, and then asked if he could see me next Friday.

Hugo doesn't say anything, and we start walking.

"We didn't kiss last night," I spit out. "It was our second date. What do you think that's about?"

Hugo slides his phone into his pocket. "Did you put it out there?"

I think about Jake and me standing in front of my door. I wanted to. It felt like he wanted to. "There was a vibe," I say.

Hugo considers this. "Maybe he's just not that into you yet." He snaps his fingers like he's just thought of something revelatory. "I bet that's something you never considered. You know it's him, but he doesn't know it's you!"

I crane my neck up to look at him. "OK, first of all, fuck you. Secondly, I feel like he is, though. I definitely feel like there's this thing between us." I take a breath in. "He was married. He told me about it last night. Maybe it was that?"

Hugo nudges my elbow to step up onto the curb to avoid a passing car. "So he's newly divorced or something?"

I shake my head. "His wife passed away. It was six or seven years ago."

Hugo rolls his neck out. "Man," he says. "Sorry for him."

I step back into the street and keep walking. "He's been through a lot. I think there's something special about him. Seriously, no bullshit. It feels, I don't know. Genuine."

Hugo stretches an arm overhead. "That's good, right?"

"Yeah," I say. "Of course."

I watch him lift the other arm and then twist his torso to the right and left, trying to crack his back.

"Is it weird when we talk about this?"

Hugo and I mostly talk about his dating life, not mine. And when we do talk about mine, it's all short-lived things. We rarely delve into feelings.

"Why?"

"Because you are bending and stretching right now like it's 1988."

"Ouch," he says, but he stops. "Yeah, I mean it's kind of weird. But I love you, so it's worth it." Hugo slings an arm over my shoulders and squeezes before letting go again.

"How was your night?" I ask.

He shrugs. "Natalie and I went to San Vicente Bungalows for, like, one drink and then came home and ordered Night Market."

"You ordered takeout on a Saturday?"

"Oh, yes, I know. I'm usually such a delinquent. Honestly, the thought of sitting at a restaurant was not that appealing. We watched *Shark Tank*, and I fell asleep at eleven."

"You hate *Shark Tank*."

Hugo shrugs. "It's not offensive."

I peer at him. His sunglasses are looped through the neck of his shirt, and his eyes look back at me like, *What?*

"You like her."

"I like Mr. Wonderful."

"No," I say. "You like her. You're acting all relationship-y."

We reach the entrance to the market. Hugo holds his hand out. *After you.*

"May I remind you," he says, "that you are the one I am currently at a farmers market with."

"Yeah, but you never would have come with me when we were dating."

Hugo wanders over to the bagel stand. "Do you want an everything?"

"Yes. Get some raisin, too."

He says something else, but I'm already halfway down the lane, pulled by a stalk of sunflowers. One thing that's nice about getting here as early as we do: if you come after ten they're all sold out.

We bring the goods back to my apartment, and I make Hugo and myself a coffee with my French press, steaming up some milk in the Nespresso. I toast two everything bagels and go about cutting up heirloom tomatoes, sautéing onions, and scrambling eggs. Murph gets some egg on his kibble, which he accepts as his due.

Hugo perches on a stool by my counter and types into his phone. "Why do I always get kicked off your Wi-Fi?" he says. A familiar refrain. He complains about it every weekend.

When we were dating, I hated his phone. I felt like it took him away from me, and I wanted all of him—so much more than I got. I remember my frustration at these moments—the mornings we would have slivers of time, maybe only minutes, to be together, and he'd be furiously answering emails before he had to run to a meeting. At the time it felt like I was being robbed of something, that he was purposefully holding us back from the sort of relationship we could have had. But maybe my need to siphon every moment was the reality that I knew our time was limited. It was always going to end, and I wanted everything I could before it was over.

Regardless, it doesn't bother me now.

Over Hugo's shoulder, I survey my apartment. Admittedly in the past few years the place has drifted from monochrome into eclectic, generously. The less kind interpretation is that I have just accumulated too much stuff. There's extra furniture from my parents, an end table that I found on the street and had refinished, even though with a coffee table there was never any room for it. And crammed behind the sofa is a credenza I had to have, because it was on massive sale at Ligne Roset. Hugo sits on one of two wooden stools I bought three years ago from a craftsman in Silver Lake, even though my dining chairs fit fine at the counter. I need to purge.

I say this to him now.

"No shit," he says without looking up. "This place is starting to resemble a hoarder's den. I'm thinking of signing you up for TNT."

"TLC."

"Yeah."

I turn my attention back to the eggs and press the toaster down one more time on the bagels.

"Are you having a half or a whole?" I ask him.

"I'm trying to lay off carbs, but realistically I'll eat both."

I hear him put down his phone. I turn back around to the counter and my coffee cup.

"So, listen," he says. He puts his elbows on the counter. "Make it happen with this guy, and then let's all go out together."

I take a sip. It's rich and hot. I like my coffee so dense it's practically a solid. "You want to double-date?"

Hugo smiles. "Definitely not. I want to take you both out for drinks and assess the situation."

I set my cup down. "You're bringing Natalie."

"She's going to get the wrong idea."

"That what? You're with her? You already are."

Hugo shakes his head. "No, that we're further down the road than we are."

"People just want connection," I say.

Hugo looks at me. "Who says I'm not connecting? Plus, she knows you're important to me."

"And that's bad?"

He shrugs. "Not at all. It's just more serious than I am with her. Meeting you is like meeting my family."

His phone dings, and he picks it back up. "How are your parents by the way? I haven't seen them since—what was it? Rosh Hashanah?"

"Passover."

"That's the one. You know your dad still wishes it had worked out with us."

I spoon some scramble onto a plate, add some sliced tomatoes and onions, and pass it to Hugo. "I don't think that's true."

"Daph, trust me. The only thing your mom wanted more than for us to get married was to marry me herself."

My parents do love Hugo but in the way all parents love tall, rich prospects. I did not consider it to be particularly individually focused.

I grab my plate, set the bagel halves in a small wooden bowl, and litter the counter with spreads—basil hummus, vegan pesto, avocado and dill crema, and a chive cream cheese.

"You spoil me," Hugo says.

"You're welcome."

We eat. The eggs are a little overcooked, but everything else is pretty good.

"Does Jake know you make meals like this?"

"Not yet."

"He'll learn."

I lay some chive cream cheese onto a half of everything bagel. "We'll see," I say.

"We're not seeing," Hugo says. "We have evidential proof."

"Do you really think it means forever?" I ask him.

The blank piece of paper has given me pause over the last day. Ever since Jake asked me what I'm looking for and we didn't kiss. I know he's a good person. It was obvious from my first time meeting him. But I'm not sure about myself. What if he wants something I can't offer?

"Don't you?"

I think about it. "Yeah," I say. "Yeah, of course."

"Well, then, there you go."

Hugo offers to wash the dishes, and I let him while I put everything back in the fridge and wipe down the counter. I have to be at my parents' house in an hour, and it's going to take me forty-five minutes to get there.

"I need to meet this guy," Hugo says as we're saying goodbye. "Let's lock it in."

Murphy walks over to Hugo at the door. He looks up at him.

"Hello," Hugo says. "I hope you're having a pleasant day, Murphy."

Murphy and Hugo get along mostly because they treat each other like polite strangers. Hugo gives Murphy all the space he requires and, in turn, Murphy doesn't ask that Hugo treat him like a dog.

I open the latch and pull at the door. Hugo gives me a quick hug and then steps outside.

"You can't use it to mark your territory, though," I say.

Murphy stands next to me in the doorway. I bend down and scoop him up. He's not particularly pleased, but he doesn't struggle.

Hugo shakes his head. “That’s ridiculous,” he says. “You’re not my territory.”

I watch him pop in his earbuds.

“You never were.”

He waves and heads down the block toward Fountain. I want to know what he means, but he’s off and running before I can ask.

Chapter Thirteen

Noah, five weeks.

I heard his Southern drawl before I ever saw him.

"That's herrr."

He made the *r* sound like it was a mile long. Waves rolling in.

"Hi," I said. "Daphne. It's nice to meet you."

I was seated at the bar of Smuggler's Cove—a tiki spot known for its rum drinks and sprawling floor plan.

"Noah," he said. "Pleasure's all mine."

He was tall—about six foot two inches with shaggy blond hair and bright blue eyes. He looked like Owen Wilson without even squinting.

Noah and I had matched on the dating app Bumble the day before. I was fresh into my San Francisco stint, staying at a hotel nearby until I found something permanent, and feeling electrified by all the specific heady freedom of being in the second half of your twenties. I had just gotten out of a long-term relationship with my college boyfriend, I was away from home for the first time in my life, and I was ready to date a Noah. Actually, I figured: I was ready to date a few Noahs.

He took a seat next to me, straddled the stool like it was a saddle, and waved over the bartender. "You up for a little adventure, Daphne?"

I was.

"Make us something strong and special," Noah said.

The bartender, a woman in her thirties with tattooed sleeves, went to work.

"You been here before?" Noah asked me.

I shook my head. "I just got here yesterday." I'd picked this bar because it was the first thing that came up on Google that was close by.

"To the city?"

"Yes. Just moved up from LA. I don't even have an apartment yet. I'm at the Hilton for the next few days." I gestured in the general direction.

"What brings you here?"

"A job," I said. I felt proud. It was my first adult one. "I'm starting at a tech company."

"Big industry out here."

"You're in school, right?"

All I knew is that he was getting his doctorate.

"I study meteorology."

"Wow," I said. "I don't think I've ever met anyone doing that."

"Loved it since I was a kid."

The bartender set down our drinks in bowls. Noah picked his

up and knocked the side of mine. I took a sip. It tasted like rum Kool-Aid with ginger. Awful.

Noah licked his lips and closed his eyes. "No shot," he said. He looked at me. Seemed to study me hard for the first time. "What do you say we go get a beer?"

"Please."

Noah put down a twenty and a ten on the counter and then took my hand. "We're just going to make a quick pit stop first."

I felt his hand. It was large and broad. My fingers felt uncharacteristically petite, hidden. I liked it.

The night was balmy and warm. It was the start of summer and endless possibility. We started walking. He did not immediately let go of my hand.

"Where are we going?" I asked.

"To see some painted ladies," he said.

We hiked up a hill. I had to tap him to slow down. I was not in the kind of shape that allowed me to traverse San Francisco. But then the street crested, and I understood what he meant. The Painted Ladies refer to seven row houses across from Alamo Square Park in San Francisco. They're beautiful. Victorian detail and in bright colors—blues and yellows and even a little red, although they've faded with time.

Painted ladies all over the city were painted during the gold rush to show off the burgeoning wealth of the city's residents. Now, they're beautiful landmarks.

We stood across the street at the park, taking them in.

"Is one of these the *Full House* house?" I asked.

"The ladies are in the opening credits. But the actual house is somewhere else."

I hear the theme song. I find it charming and out of character that he knows this. I expected a nonresponse.

"They call them Postcard Row or the Seven Sisters," he said. "I'm not over here too much. But when I am I like to give 'em a look."

"How come?" I asked. It seemed out of character for him. But then again, everything about Noah seemed out of character. A Texan in the city by the bay with a penchant for studying the sky.

Noah laughed. It was the first time I'd heard him laugh. It was wholly original. The kind you want to record for a ringtone. Later I would look back on that and think it was the moment. The moment I decided to go on whatever ride he was selling tickets for.

"I like to see what a place is known for. Helps me see what a place is about."

Growing up in LA I always thought the tourists who groped for their cameras down Rodeo Drive or took eager bus tours to the best view of the Hollywood sign were, in a word, desperate. I was embarrassed by their visors and fanny packs and clear out-of-water attitude. Who would be that earnest on purpose? Who would let it show? It was grotesque. But now that I was new somewhere—in some ways for the very first time—I saw it. All the wonder that comes from seeing something that is so known, so recognized. For witnessing a place's celebrity.

The things that will outlive us.

"And if you look up, on a night like tonight you can even see the dipper." Noah cupped the back of my head with his palm. I felt it. I leaned back and looked up. The sky was splayed out like a screen, like an open road.

"You study stars," I said, my head still back.

He moved behind me. I felt his body, his other hand found my hip.

"I study the atmosphere," he said. "I study why we can see the stars."

I picked my head back up. He dropped his hand from my hip. All at once I realized how far I was from home. How unknown this life was. How I was just making introductions.

"Let's get a little liquid," he said.

We went to a local pub for beers and bags of potato chips, and when Noah finally walked me back to the Hilton—tipsy and swollen from salt—I felt something rise up in me. A want. A hunger for something different. Whatever he was, whatever he had to offer, I wanted more of it that night.

"You have plans this weekend?" he asked, standing on the welcome mat. The automated doors opened and closed, waiting for me to make a decision. In or out.

"You're the only person I know in San Francisco," I told him.

"Well, if that isn't a call to action, I don't know what is."

When I got inside there was a receptionist waving me over. She handed me an envelope. "This came for you," she said.

Five weeks.

I felt my skin prick up with goose bumps. I felt alive. It was the only thing I wanted to feel. Breathing. Vibrant. Present.

Five weeks. I'd take it.

Chapter Fourteen

Honey, listen, I need you to bring me over a dozen doughnuts from that place on Third that makes them gluten-free. Amy is coming, and if I don't have a gluten-free substitute for everything on my table I won't hear the end of it."

"Why a dozen?" I'm balancing in a towel, water running down my back and onto the tile floor.

She clears her throat through the phone. "Suppose they're good?"

"Call in the order, and I'll grab them on my way over."

"OK, mummashanna. Wear something nice. You never know."

"Mom, it's brunch at your house."

"People have friends! And drive carefully. No rushing."

She hangs up, and I flip my hair into a towel, drying off my body, moisturizing, and then folding into a giant terry-cloth robe.

I try not to look at myself too often naked. All the freckles and scars and birthmarks expanding and contracting. I read in a magazine one time that every woman should spend five minutes a day staring at her naked body. I'd rather hurl myself off a balcony.

I run a brush through my hair and then add some product to it. It will still dry straight—it always does—but if I'm lucky, the right amount of air can give me a windswept look, like I've just been caught in some light convertible play.

There's a vintage floral dress I bought recently at Decades on Melrose hanging on the door of my closet. It's white, with tiny blue flowers and cap sleeves. I put it on, pulling a cream cable-knit cardigan over it and sliding into some brown loafers. I add minimal makeup and walk out the door.

The drive down Sunset is hit or miss with traffic on the weekends, but today I hit a glide, and I'm at my parents' doorstep in half an hour, which is practically a record.

When I was growing up we lived on the border of Brentwood and the Pacific Palisades on a tree-lined street. My parents now live much deeper, past the Palisades Village, a Mickey Mouse shopping mall that looks like it belongs in Stepford Wives, California—the sequel. There is an Erewhon, which is the best upscale grocery store in all of California. The strawberries are twelve dollars, but they're life-changing.

Their new home is modest. Three bedrooms, single level. It's an old house, built in the seventies, with stone steps leading up to the front door. My dad greets me when I get there.

"Chicken," he says. "You're here."

My father is a short and trim man, with a goatee and a full head of gray hair. He's been calling me "chicken" since I was a baby, when he says I came out looking like a fresh piece of poultry.

"Hey, Papa," I say. I present the doughnuts, and he takes them out of my hands.

"Your mother," he says, shaking his head. "Come on."

He carries the box in one hand and puts an arm around me with the other.

"How was your morning?" he asks me. "You feeling good?"

"Yep. Hugo and I went to the farmers market and had breakfast."

My father eyes me and drops his voice. "You already ate?"

"Don't worry," I say. "I won't tell her. And there's plenty of appetite where that came from."

We enter the kitchen to reveal my mother, apron on, brown curls in a clip, her zaftig figure in black pants and a blue sweater, bustling around the kitchen like she's hosting Thanksgiving.

"Oh, Daphne. Hi. Moshe, why are you holding them like that?"

She snatches the doughnut box from my father, where it has been tucked under his arm thoughtlessly, the insides, I'm sure, in crumbs.

She opens the box on the counter.

"Moshe," she says. "They slid."

"Call the authorities, Debra!" my father bellows. "They slid!"

My mother smiles. This is their thing. My mom sweats everything, and my father calls her out on it. It works, perhaps, most importantly, because she lets him.

"You look gorgeous," my mother tells me. She puts her hands on the sides of my face. They're warm. They're always warm. "How is my love?"

"Good, Mom. Fine!"

She goes to the cabinet and gets a plate down and hands it to me, motioning to the doughnuts. I start lifting them out of their box and onto the plate.

The counter is cluttered with food. Bagels, a tray of lox, cut onions, tomatoes, capers, and cucumbers. There's a fruit plate, and a basket of pastries, some of which I can tell my mother baked.

She taught me how to fry an egg, set a table, chop a scallion. Our taste buds are different—my mother prefers the traditional food she grew up with, and I like a little more spice—but whatever I know how to make, I learned from her.

"You're hungry?" she asks.

I look at my father. He winks.

"Starving," I say.

The front door opens, and Joan, my parents' neighbor, comes in carrying a bouquet of wild roses with a wet paper towel wrapped around its base.

"Deb, I burnt the hamantaschen and I—" She rounds the corner. She has on silk pants and a linen button-down, and her silver hair hangs in strings around her shoulders. "Oh, hi, honey." She kisses me on the cheek. Joan always smells like vegetable soup, no matter the time of day or year. "How are you?"

"Keeping the bats at bay," I tell her.

Joan frowns, and my mother takes the flowers.

"The roses are really going off," Joan says. "You wouldn't believe it. I have yellow ones now, too. Lance told me they only bloom in the summer, but you get a sunny day around here and all of a sudden they're lining the wall."

The roses she has brought us today are the lightest shade of pink, rimmed with bright neon at their edges. They're beautiful.

"I'll have to come get some," my mother says. "Mine have suffered with the drought this year."

I think about telling her they looked gorgeous outside: plump and bright and full—but the roses seem to be an unspoken point of contention between my mother and Joan. I leave it.

The doorbell rings. My father calls, "Coming!"

Once every other month, my mother throws a brunch for her friends at Kehillat Israel, the reconstructionist temple she and my father belong to in the Pacific Palisades. We've always been reform, but over the years my mother got more and more progressive, and now their temple has things like namaSHVITZ yoga, bead blessings, and curiously uniform feelings about Israel.

My father comes into the kitchen with Marty and Dox, and Irvin and the Other Debra. The Other Debra is not my mother's favorite person, but my father loves Irvin (as does she, as do I), so she tolerates her.

"Welcome, everyone!" my mother calls. "Onto the patio. Out of the kitchen!"

My mother air-kisses them all and shoos them out. Joan and I stay behind with her.

"Any men?" Joan asks me.

My mother makes a bristling noise but doesn't turn around from the stove, where she is now preparing a frittata with caramelized onions.

I consider it, then: "Kind of."

At this she whips around.

"His name is Jake," I say. "We've only been out twice." What's the difference? The paper says what the paper says. I might as well give them something juicy to chew on while I'm here.

"What does he do?" my mother asks.

"He's a studio exec," I say. "He's not very tall, I'm sorry, but he seems pretty sweet."

Joan clasps her hands together. "Oh, to be young!" she says.

Joan's husband passed away three years ago from pancreatic cancer. My mother sat shiva the whole week with her and cooked for the month following. We loved Hal. He was warm and hearty—a big, burly man who wasn't shy about throwing his arms around her or anyone who walked through their door. They had two sons together, both of whom live in New York. There was an era in which Joan was hell-bent on getting me together with her eldest, David, but he always had a girlfriend—who five years ago became his wife. Joan still tells me that maybe someday they'll get divorced.

"What else?" my mother asks. "How did you meet?"

"Kendra set us up." I look at Joan. "My friend from work."

"Is he Jewish?"

It's a good question. His name is Jake Green, but it's hard to say. "I think so," I tell her.

A timer goes off, and my mother takes some sizzling potatoes out of the oven. "Joannie, take the fruit out, will you?"

Joan grabs the platter and does as she's told. I hold a ceramic plate underneath the potato tray as my mother scoops them off.

"How is Hugo?" she asks.

It's true what he thinks, my mother does love him.

"He's good," I say. "He stopped by today."

"Doesn't he have a girlfriend?"

"No? Maybe. It's Hugo. I never really know."

My mother smiles. "He is handsome."

I consider Hugo's sweat-laden running clothes this morning. He does even make them look good. "He is," I say. "The problem is that he knows it."

Joan comes back into the kitchen. "What's next?"

My mother points to the doughnut tray. "Those are for Amy," she says. "Where is Amy?"

Joan shrugs and brings out the bagels.

"It's not such a problem," my mother says. "Your father knows I'm smart; it works."

"Hugo knows *he's* handsome, not that I am, there's a difference."

My mother comes up to me. I see the lines around her eyes, her hair that she's beginning to let go gray. "Mummashanna," she says, taking my face in her hands once again. "It's not attractive to state the obvious."

Chapter Fifteen

Irina is in New York the following week to oversee a press photo shoot, and I mostly work from home. But Tuesday I go to her house in Laurel Canyon to check the mail and water the plants and fax over a new version of a script with my notes—Irina is old-school. I ask Kendra if she wants to come with me. Kendra is now the head of development for a showrunner on the ABC lot, and is always at work in Burbank, but today she has a doctor's appointment on the west side in the morning, and we decide to meet at Irina's house.

Kendra pulls up in her navy-blue Jeep Cherokee, the Chicks blaring. She is tall—six feet on a bad day—and she's got a mass of curly black hair. She wears jeans almost exclusively, and most of her T-shirts are cropped—I used to think it was by necessity, but now I know it's by design. She's got great abs, so I get it.

I think about our first meeting. I didn't immediately think we would be friends. In fact, I assumed we wouldn't. We would overlap for the time it took to train me, and then she would move on. I wanted her to stay just long enough to teach me all the logistics. I had no intention of reinventing the wheel with Irina. I just wanted to know what kind of oil the machine preferred and how to keep securing it.

The first day in Irina's office Kendra gave me a big hug. I come from an affectionate family, but it had been a while since I'd experienced that level of unselfconscious display from someone I wasn't related to or sleeping with.

"Welcome," she said. "This job is a lot of fun."

Later she'd tell me about the hard parts—Irina could be temperamental; the hours were sometimes very long; I'd deal with a lot of personalities and no one had any patience. But I always appreciated that she opened with joy. That's who Kendra is. Fun first.

Irina's house is situated on Lookout Mountain, right at the summit of Laurel Canyon. It's an old house, built in the fifties, with a sunken living room, lots of wood and little light, and a neutral palette. The back of the house has an addition, though, with floor-to-ceiling windows that look out over Los Angeles. She has one of the most stunning views I've seen. There is a terraced lawn beyond the house, and a black stone pool in the yard. It's a sexy house, a house with character, one that screams Old Hollywood, although Irina would hate the world *old*. She's fifty-eight, but no one is allowed to say that number out loud or put it down in writing unless it's a health form.

"You don't know what it's like for women in this town," she tells me often. "The parents on teen shows are in their thirties."

I often remind her she's not an actress, and that producing is a different skill set, and that standards of age when it comes to beauty are changing, but she always pushes back.

"No one wants to make a movie with someone they don't want to fuck."

I un-alarm the house, and Kendra goes to get some water for the flowers—the orchids take one ice cube of spring water, and the fiddle-leaf fig trees get eight ounces of tap, every two weeks. This is the third fiddle leaf I've killed, and every time their leaves start to turn brown for frustratingly vague reasons I feel like a murderer.

Irina's cat, Moses, comes out from the bathroom and nuzzles up against Kendra's leg.

"Oh, hi, baby." Kendra scoops him up and cuddles him into her. "Who is looking after you?"

"Penelope," I say.

Penelope is Irina's on-again, off-again girlfriend, who was once her wife. "Great with cats, terrible with plants," according to Irina.

"What cycle are we in with that?"

There was no car in the driveway, so I know she's not currently home.

"Off?" I venture. They usually seem happier when they're not together, and lately they've been pretty happy.

I check the mail—some junk, some household bills, a few screeners—and give Moses a healthy scoop of kibble, just in case.

There is a framed photo of patron saint Patti Smith over the mantel in the living room, and an area comprised entirely of sheepskin, fur throws, and pillows that Irina calls "the playpen" to the right of it. Den of iniquity meets cozy, basically. This house just constantly looks like it's trying to get into your pants.

I love it here. I remember the first time I walked in, I thought: *This is what a point of view looks like.*

When Irina is in New York, she is usually scheduled socially up to the actual minute, so as long as I remember to make her dinner reservations at Babbo, she doesn't mind if we take a bit of a breather in her absence. She'll never call and ask what I'm doing just for the hell of it. If she's taken care of, and the business is humming, that's all that matters.

The last plant is a palm in Irina's closet, which is a room all its own. There are mirrored sliding doors on every wall, and in the center is an island, with a glass top, and drawers on the sides. It's a masterpiece, the crowning jewel of this home, and not just because of its size, which is enormous, but because of what's in it. Irina has archives from every decade—incredible seventies sequins, Laura Ashley sundresses from the eighties. There is custom Givenchy and the entire line of Prada's women's wear from the year 1992. She has at least fifty black blazers. It's heaven.

"I love it in here," Kendra says. She leans against the counter. "You know she once told me I could borrow the tulle skirt for my cousin's wedding? It didn't fit, though."

Irina has *the* tulle skirt—the very same one Sarah Jessica Parker a.k.a. Carrie Bradshaw wears in the opening credits of *Sex and the City*.

"Yes," I tell Kendra. "You've only mentioned it to me fifty times."

Kendra fingers an Hermès silk neck scarf that's hung with a dozen others on a little display on top of the island.

"I miss it sometimes," she says.

"What?"

"Working here. How unexpected it always was."

"Irina loves you," I tell Kendra. "She'd probably let you live in this closet if you wanted to."

Kendra smiles. "Yes," she says. "But things change, you know? It's different now than it used to be."

"With you two?"

Kendra shrugs. "It used to drive me crazy, how she'd call me on the weekends at all hours, but sometimes I miss the drama."

"I feel like there's less drama, in general," I say. The last time Irina got truly worked up it was about a legitimate scheduling conflict on a film shoot—not a celery juice. And it was at 11:00 a.m. on a Wednesday.

I water the palm and then clap my hands together. "I'm starving," I say. "Let's eat."

Half an hour later we're seated at Art's Deli on Ventura in the valley. We haven't been here in ages, at least a year. But during those weeks where Kendra was training me we came all the time. We'd go to work, and then at five or six or seven, whenever we'd finish, we'd drive over the hill and sit in a red booth and order—a Reuben for Kendra, and a BLT with coleslaw for me. They have giant soda glasses—sixty-four ounces—and we'd sit for at least two hours, debriefing on the day, picking at cold fries.

"Ah, memories," Kendra says, sliding in. We're handed thick plastic menus, but we don't even look at them.

"Wait," Kendra says, once the waitress—Gretchen—leaves.

Gretchen is probably in her mid-forties, with a wide but impatient smile. We recognize her, but she doesn't recognize us.

"I haven't even asked you about how it's going with Jake."

Reflexively, I feel my face break into a smile.

"That good?"

"We've only been out twice," I say. "There isn't a lot to tell."

"Bullshit," Kendra says. "You don't get this"—she loops her finger in the air around my face—"stupid."

I have never told Kendra about the notes. Not because I think she'd think I was crazy—because she would—but because I never tell anyone. For forever, it was my private joke with the universe, my little behind-the-scenes snapshot. I didn't tell anyone because it felt like it would be breaking a promise. Like exposing this anomaly to air might oxidize it, and then I might never receive another note again. That the spell would be broken.

To date, Hugo is the only one who knows.

"It's true," I say. "I have a good feeling about him. He's sweet, and really smart." I pause. "Did you know his wife?"

Kendra shakes her head. "No. It was before I met him."

I nod.

"He's been through a lot," Kendra says. "But I think it's made him kinder. He has a maturity a lot of men don't. You can just sense it in him. He's a real grown-up."

"I know what you mean," I say.

"We should all do something soon," Kendra says.

Kendra's husband is a man named Joel. They got married last year on the beach in Malibu. Sunset, twenty people, a lace doily for a veil and Bob Marley on the car sound system. Her sister officiated, and afterward we went to Geoffrey's on the ocean and drank cold beer and warm red wine, ate oysters, and listened to the waves crash up against the rocks below us. It was perfect, and so very Kendra.

The thing about Joel is that he's not the friendliest, or better:

the most outgoing. Maybe that's a little too harsh, and maybe the comparison to Kendra is just extreme. He's always been nice to me, but he's a software engineer and way more comfortable in rooms alone than in any larger conversation. He usually encourages girls' nights, and resists anything involving a dinner table outside their home. I respect their relationship because it always appears—at least from the outside—that they let each other be exactly who they are.

He loves to hike; you'll never find her on the trail. He's a true pescatarian, and Kendra lives off hamburgers. But they balance each other.

"Joel has met Jake before," she says. "He liked him."

I unstick my shirt from the leather booth. It gives off a suctioning sound.

"Do you ever miss being single?" I ask her.

Kendra thinks for a moment. "I honestly never thought I'd get married. I never really wanted to, the whole thing seemed kind of stale and obvious." She shrugs. "And then I met Joel."

"That's not an answer."

Kendra smiles. "Oh, but it is."

Our food arrives then. The bacon is crispy, the lettuce is wilted but fresh, and the tomatoes are sweet. There's nothing fussy about it, just the basics. I missed this place.

"So in other words, no."

"In other words, eat your food," Kendra says, taking a bite.

Chapter Sixteen

On Friday I go to Jake's apartment for dinner.

"I cook," he said when he called Wednesday. "Not well, but enough. Would you like to come over for dinner?"

I put on my favorite AGOLDE jeans and a white sleeveless turtleneck that sits just below my naval. I tie up some strappy python heels I'll likely have to kick off after an hour, and grab a black clutch. I survey myself in the mirror. Not bad. My hair is a little straggled, and my face looks slightly pale. I swipe a bronzer brush across my cheeks, yank my top down a little closer to my jeans, grab a pair of gold hoops, and make my way out the door.

Jake lives in an apartment in a high-rise on Wilshire Corridor, which immediately strikes me as both hilarious and incongruent. For one, the median age of residents in Wilshire Corridor is probably around eighty-four. For another, it feels off-brand for Jake, what little I know of him. I pictured him in a small complex in Culver City, with a shared garden. Wilshire Corridor is almost like living in New York.

An overanxious doorman greets me in a wide marbled lobby. "Miss? Can I help you?"

"I'm here to see Jake Green?"

He sends me up to the seventeenth floor, and when the elevator doors open I see Jake's head poking out of door 17F, trying to keep a dog at bay.

"This is Saber," he says. "He's a little overly friendly."

I crouch down to greet a bulldog mix who is excitedly shuffling behind Jake's legs. "Can I pet him?"

Jake nods, holding his collar. "He loves attention. But be prepared to be slobbered on."

I pat Saber's head and he rears his chin up, greeting my hand.

"Oh, hi," I say. "Hi. Hi." I look up at Jake. "My dog doesn't really like human contact, this is so nice."

Jake tugs on his collar. "Come on," he says. "Inside."

I follow them through the doorway, and then Jake holds out a toy to Saber, and donkey-carrots him to his bed. Once Saber is seated, Jake lets him have the toy. The dog immediately starts drooling all over the plastic cylinder.

"It's a peanut butter dispenser," Jake says. "It keeps him occupied for hours." He smiles at me then—a warm, welcoming smile.

"You look wonderful," he says.

I feel myself blush. "Thank you."

Jake is wearing a white-and-blue button-down and dark jeans. He's barefoot, and his shirt is untucked, the sleeves pushed up to reveal his freckled forearms. All at once I'm met with the intoxicating scent of butter and garlic.

"White or red?" Jake asks me.

"Red," I say.

"You got it."

His apartment is spacious, with a stunning view of LA. From this high up, you can see a good chunk of the city. There is a sectional couch by the wall, a television across from it, and, around the corner, a galley kitchen. Jake disappears there, and I follow him.

The kitchen looks brand-new—all stainless steel appliances, and a small, round table for four sits off to the left-hand side. I take a seat while Jake opens the wine.

"How long have you been here for?" I ask him.

"About a year," he says. "No, maybe almost two, now."

"I have to ask," I say. "What made you end up in Wilshire Corridor?"

The cork comes out with a pop. "Whatever do you mean?" Jake says with a grin.

He picks up the bottle, and I hear the wine slosh against the glass.

"It's not exactly a youthful zip code."

Jake laughs. "I'll claim ignorance on that front. Honestly, the building was having a great deal, and it was close to work. At the time, it's what mattered to me."

"Pragmatic."

He hands me the wine. I take a sip. Rich and full.

"It turns out I like it, though," he says. "My neighbors bake all the time, they're always home to water my plants or feed Saber if I'm running late, and whenever someone dies, there's the Brisket Brigade."

My eyes go wide, and I practically spit out my wine. "What do you know about the Brisket Brigade?"

My grandmother was fond of the phrase. She said in her later years, whenever a man's wife would die, women would show up in droves with brisket in the hopes of being his next wife. Whoever made the best brisket won his hand.

"Only my lived experience," Jake says. "They always throw me the leftovers. You know kugel freezes very well."

"Are you Jewish?" I ask him.

Jake smiles. "More now than I've ever been before."

I feel a warmth spread out through my limbs, although if it's the wine or the revelation of—what? Familiarity? I cannot say. It was always important to my parents that I be with someone Jewish. Not because they are particularly religious people—they lived together for seven years before they got married, and the only time either one of my parents covers their heads is in the rain. But tradition is important to them.

"You never want to be a stranger in your own family," my mother used to say.

Jake raises his glass to mine. "To Friday," he says. We clink. "Here, I want you to see the view."

The doors are sliders, and he opens them and then holds his arm out for me to step onto the terrace.

It's cool out, from way up here, the wind is blowing, and I hug my arms to my chest as I look out over the city.

"I used to think LA was just a place I saw in movies," Jake says. "I thought it was devoid of any character—how could somewhere so beautiful also be interesting? It wasn't until I had been living here for a few years that I realized it's not all Technicolor. There's a lot that makes this place artistic and cultural and relevant, I think."

"It's all I know," I tell him. "I've never lived anywhere else for more than a few months."

But I do understand what he means. When I was growing up, LA was full of phonies, or at least that's how it often felt to me. A city of people who drove Ferraris and then went home to dilapidated apartments in Burbank. Everything was for show. But Los Angeles has changed, or maybe I've just grown up. I see now it's not one specific thing. There really is no unified narrative. Los Angeles is many things. Full of life and nature and a myriad of experiences, just like everywhere else. The thing that differentiates it, maybe, is the surplus of hope—the dreams both tightly held and scattered.

"In high school it definitely felt like you just had to be rich and thin to be important," I say. "But I think that's changing. There's a really amazing art scene, downtown is having a renaissance." I point eastward. "There's a lot to love about it here that doesn't include the weather or 'the industry' or a plastic surgeon's office."

Jake touches down to the railing beside me. "But the weather is also pretty great."

We are silent for a moment—taking in the surrounding sounds, the low drum of traffic below, the feeling of the open-air breeze.

"This was the first place I lived in alone," Jake says. "Or, the first place I picked on my own, I should say. I think that's part of what attracted me to the place. I never feel alone here. There's always something going on." He jerks up from the railing. "Shit! Be right back."

From the balcony I see him dash into the kitchen and open the oven. I turn back out toward the city.

When I was young I used to want to live in New York in a building just like this one. I wanted to be high in the sky, way above ordinary life. Somewhere I could get some perspective, where problems would seem small and petty and pocket-size. Somewhere untouchable.

The closest I ever got was that night in Stuart's apartment.

Jake returns. "Question for you," he says. "You prefer rice to be hard and also gummy at the same time, right?"

I walk in toward him. "Let me see," I say. "Rice happens to be my specialty."

The rice gets salvaged, and Jake makes a truly impressive Moroccan chicken and Greek salad. It's all delicious. The tomatoes are ripe and juicy, and the chicken is crisped to perfection. Jake sets down a plate of olives, too, and we spit out their stone centers into a small ceramic bowl.

Afterward we leave the dishes piled high in the sink, refill our wineglasses, and take them back out onto the balcony. The city is lit now. The whole view plays out in a string of colored lights. Sparkling high-rises, the glittered snake of traffic. Palm trees dot the industrial horizon.

Jake turns to me, putting his wineglass down on the table below us. I feel the spark of energy between us, the same pull that was present at Pace nearly a week ago now. I get the feeling that he's taking it slow for a reason—that the more intentional this is, the sturdier. But I also feel impatient.

"Hey," he says. He touches my elbow. "I want to kiss you."

My fingers tighten around my wineglass.

"Is that OK?" he asks me.

I look at him. Even in the darkness I can tell his cheeks are rosy from the wine—not because of the color but because his whole face has a moonlike quality now. Round and lit.

"Do it," I say.

He takes my wineglass out of my hand and sets it down next to his. I hear the clink of glass on glass.

Then he takes both my elbows in his palms. He runs his hands up to my shoulders, and then he leans his face closer—and kisses me. We are pretty much eye to eye at this height, especially because I still have on heels. His lips land softly on mine, and I feel that familiar hovering sensation, the millisecond of stillness before a fall.

And then his hand reaches tentatively for my waist. It's timid—no, it's seeking. It's asking: *Is this OK? Here? Now? Me?*

He pulls back after a moment. His face is so honest I think I can see the words scrolled there before he says them.

"We should do this again," he says. He's smiling. Even in the surrounding darkness, I can see it.

We're moving toward something softly—like a cat, whisper quiet. I want to call it graceful.

I nod. I reach back up for his face in answer.

Chapter Seventeen

Dating Hugo was like being on a Sizzler ride. It was thrilling and nauseating and often felt like I couldn't catch my breath, or see what was right in front of me. We were moving too fast.

We'd been dating for just under a month when he asked me if I wanted to go to Big Sur with him.

I was wary—of him, his past, and the paper—I knew our time was limited, and I could also see the strength of my feelings, how quickly they were growing. I wanted Hugo all the time. His presence, his attention, even his approval. I found myself often embellishing anecdotes from work I thought he would find charming, or doing research about topics he'd mentioned just to impress him. I wanted him to laugh, I wanted to be the person who made him open his mouth and say yes. With Hugo it felt a little like I'd won a prize—but one that I was always in danger of losing. I wanted to keep him, which meant, I wanted to keep his attention. In those early, hazy days I would forget—for very long stretches of time—where this was all headed.

I had never been super attached in love. I'd experienced heartbreak only once, in college. We met our junior year, and were together for two years and two months. Long enough to fall in love. Long enough to think it might not matter. But of course, it did.

I boarded Murphy at Wagville, packed a bag, and Hugo picked me up in a black Ferrari for our weekend away.

"Seriously?" I asked when I saw him.

"I'm just trying it out," he said. "Embarrassing?"

"Deeply."

Hugo got out and came around to my side. He surveyed the car. "I agree." Then he turned his attention to me. "Hi," he said. "Damn, I missed you."

Being with Hugo felt like having the sun shining down on you and you alone. When I was with him I felt wrapped in this vortex of warmth—like a greenhouse of flowers in full bloom. Everything was hot and bright and growing.

"Hi."

He kissed me. Swooped down and planted one on my lips, and then my cheek, and then back on my lips. He squeezed me closer to him. It made me giggle. I giggled with Hugo. I could never remember giggling before. It felt moronic. It felt precious—like I was something to be held and tended.

"Ready?" he asked.

I handed him my overnight bag. He'd told me to pack light, and I had—now I saw why.

Hugo put my bag in the trunk of the car, which was in the hood—and tiny, about two feet by three. The bag just fit.

I climbed inside, and he closed the door for me, then got in himself.

He then gestured to the center console. Two takeaway coffee cups sat in their containers. "Yours is the one in front," he said. "Decaf cappuccino, extra foam."

I felt something inside my chest lift. "Yes."

"The radio is your responsibility," he said. "I have no taste in music."

This I hadn't heard before. We were still getting to know each other. I loved discovering the details. Every single thing I learned about Hugo felt worthy of notation and study—there was no filler. He would lean his head closer to me when I touched the back of his neck. If you asked him a question, the response you normally got was "absolutely." He would only wear V-neck shirts if they were in gray. He was meticulous about his hair. He never texted with emojis.

"What does that mean?" I said. "You have no taste or no interest?"

He glanced at me as he turned on the engine. "Astute. What's the difference?"

I thought about it. "Are you saying if you had interest you'd have taste?"

Hugo pulled onto the road. I saw the side of his face curl up. "My ego is not that big."

I cleared my throat and clicked on the radio. "Yes, it is."

The drive took us five hours flat. Hugo drove fast, pushing one hundred on the freeway. By the time we got to the coast I barely noticed as he flew around the turns.

"Look over my shoulder," he said. "This is some of the most beautiful stretch of road in the world."

The ocean crashed to the left below us, and the cliffs—increasingly more jagged—made me feel like we had crossed over into Ireland. Somewhere foreign and magical where it was always winter. About an hour in, my cell phone lost service. I held it out to him.

"Just you and me," he said. "Any regrets?"

"You without a phone?" I said. "I cannot think of anything better."

He reached across and squeezed my knee.

The Post Ranch Inn is a forty-room hotel built into the California coastline. We parked, and I got out, stretching my legs and hinging at the waist. I felt the blood rush back into my limbs.

Hugo unloaded the car as I looked around. The serene beauty of the place was physical—I could feel my body relaxing with every step I took. Even the air was different—it smelled like rain and pines and lavender. It felt pristine, too. It wasn't mixed with exhaust and chemicals. Nothing there felt contaminated.

We were shown to our room—a bungalow hanging over the ocean with its own private terrace—complete with lounge chairs and a bubbling hot tub. The interior looked like a chic, woodsy cabin—all cherrywood and exposed beams with a steel fireplace, already lit.

"This is heaven," I said.

Behind me I heard Hugo thank our bellhop, and then the close of the door.

"I'm glad you like it. It's one of my favorite places in the world."

I turned around to see Hugo lifting champagne out of an ice bucket. I heard the cork pop. I untied my sweater from around my waist and slipped it over my head.

"Here we go." Hugo came outside carrying two glasses. I took one out of his hands. We clinked. I took a sip. It was icy and sweet—delicious.

"It's crazy to think this is just five hours away," I said.

Hugo smiled. "It's a different universe, right?"

"Let's stay here."

Hugo leaned over and kissed my shoulder. I felt his teeth on my sweater. "Now," he said. "I have to show you around."

"The hotel?"

Hugo took the glass out of my hand and placed it down on the ledge of the hot tub. "Our room."

He took my hand and led me back inside.

Part of the excitement and allure of this trip was simple: we hadn't had sex yet.

We'd fooled around, heavily made out—I'd even spent the night. But sex hadn't happened yet. Part of it was that we hadn't seen each other that frequently—Hugo was always traveling, and work for me was particularly time intensive—and part of it was that the previous week, when all systems were a go, I got my period. Fine for down-the-road sex, but first time felt aggressive.

"This is the sitting room, complete with two seventies-inspired couches." Hugo maneuvered me by the maroon loungers, and the glass and chrome coffee table between them.

"Very groovy."

"This is our breakfast nook."

Two wooden chairs sat beside a small table in the corner that had a basket on it filled with fruits and nuts and what looked to be some kind of dessert bread.

"And this is—I'm blanking on what you call it . . ." Hugo turned to me with a deadly grin, pointing to the bed.

"The thing for sleeping?"

He slipped an arm around my waist, and leaned his mouth down to my neck. "Hell no."

I reached up to meet him, and he planted a kiss right below my ear. I felt myself go gelatinous in his arms. I sat down on the bed, and then scooted back, pulling him with me.

I wanted to have sex with Hugo, so much so that I felt like I had been driving it these past few weeks. But I was also scared about what it might do to us. I was in deeper than I should have been; I could feel it. And I was angry at myself for it, too. If I were my friend, I'd be telling me that men like this don't change, that he was momentarily infatuated with me and that it would fade, just like all the others had. That whatever was between us would not prove to be special.

I didn't need a friend, I had a paper saying it for me.

The problem was, my body refused to believe it.

"This is all I could think about on the drive up here," Hugo said. "It's all I've been thinking about for weeks."

My mind flashed, briefly, on that acting class parking lot. Cassandra at the door. Was it possible that the only reason Hugo was still interested in me was that we hadn't yet had sex? And that once we did, the spell would be broken? I thought about Stuart, all those years ago.

He dug his fingers into the small of my back and I exhaled out against him. Who could care.

Hugo moved his mouth from my neck to my collarbone. He dipped his lips into the space there, threading his tongue along the bone. I swallowed.

"Here, sit up," he said.

I did, and he reached down to the hem of my sweater. I helped him take it off, the shirt underneath came with it.

I had worn one of my best bras—a hot-pink lace affair with a middle clasp, but Hugo didn't even seem to notice. His fingers trailed lightly down my chest then, hovering at the spot right over my left breast. His fingers were cold, I shimmied away from him.

"What's wrong?" he asked. "What is that?"

I shook my head. "Nothing, just cold."

Hugo lifted the duvet from where it was tucked into the sides of the bed and held it up. While I got inside, he took his shirt and jeans off.

The blankets were crisp and cool, and I could feel the warmth of my skin against them. Hugo climbed in beside me and then took my body into his arms. "You're freezing," he said.

I could feel the goose bumps prick up like needles.

He started running his hands down my arms. First gently, and then more firmly. I turned so my chest was pressed up against his—skin on skin on skin. I could feel his breathe on my neck. He was warm—not just warm, hot. I moved myself even closer to him. He felt like a heat lamp. I wanted to be underneath him. No, more than that. I wanted him to take off his skin, and I wanted to breathe beneath it, that's how close I wanted to be.

He wrapped his hands tightly around my back.

"Better?" he asked.

"Much."

I pulled back just enough to see his face. His eyes were open—big pools of liquid gold. I felt like if I fell into them, I'd be trapped in lava.

I reached my fingertips up and touched his cheeks. And then I leaned my face up and kissed him. His lips were cool and soft and buttery. Hugo pulled me back and looked at me.

"You're really special to me," he said. He traced a hand over my cheek. "Really special."

I wanted to believe it. I wanted so much to believe it. Because it felt so good being there with him, right up against him, that close.

But I also knew I shouldn't. *Three months.* I saw the number in my head, like a serpent.

"I bet you tell everyone that," I said.

He smiled a slow, languid smile. "Not even close."

Chapter Eighteen

Irina returns from New York Wednesday late morning, complaining about travel bloat and insisting on a water cleanse that's supposed to last twenty-four hours. Around four she asks me if I want to order pad thai, extra spicy, extra vegetables.

"Do you have plans?" she says, standing in her kitchen, silk robe–clad, opening a bottle of merlot.

"No," I say honestly. Jake and I had lunch yesterday, Kendra is home with her husband, and Hugo is in New York until Friday. This makes me pause. I used to have friends, but now, if it's not for a wedding, bachelorette party, or birthday, I rarely see anyone. Part of it is that by the time we made it to thirty most of my friends moved away—to New York, San Francisco, Seattle, DC. Wednesday night drinks were replaced with weekly texts. Some of them—most of them—have babies, now. It's hard to hold on to people the older we get. Life looks different for everyone, and you have to keep choosing one another. You have to make a conscious effort to say, over and over again, "You." Not everyone makes that choice. Not everyone can.

Irina gestures toward a stool at the counter. "You want to stay?"

Hanging out with Irina is like hanging out with a very glamorous, very self-serving therapist. She wants to buy you dinner, a designer bag, and listen to your problems, which she will cast as gossip from across the couch.

"Sure."

She takes down another wineglass and pours, then sets the drink in front of me.

"So," she says. "Kendra tells me you're seeing someone."

I cough out a laugh. "When will I learn your motives are never altruistic?"

"Hopefully never," Irina says. "But now that we're here, tell me everything." She comes to sit beside me at the counter. "Shrimp fried rice?"

I nod.

"And some summer rolls, so we can say we tried."

She types in an order and discards the iPad on the counter. "What's his deal?"

"He's nice."

"Nice?"

"Nice is underrated."

"I'm almost twenty years older than you—"

I raise my eyebrows but don't say anything.

"So I can assure you, nice just means bad in bed."

"I don't think that's true," I say.

"You don't think or you know?"

"We haven't slept together yet."

Irina lifts her wineglass at me. "I'm telling you. It's been a while, but: kind spirit, limp dick."

"I'm adding that quote to your bio."

She smiles. "If you're happy I'm happy, sweetheart. You deserve only the best."

I take a small sip of wine. "Thank you. How's Penelope?"

Irina shakes her head. "Sometimes I feel like I'm sixty fucking years old having the relationship of someone twenty-five."

"Isn't that a good thing?"

"Not if you're sixty fucking years old."

I try not to think about aging. At least, not aging in relationships. Part of the beauty of the paper is that it allows me to be present. To not plan ahead too far, not further than specified. Until now.

"I guess," I say. "I haven't really thought about it too much."

Irina puts a hand over mine. I can feel the cold metal of her silver cocktail rings on my skin. "Oh, sweetheart," she says. "I'm sorry. Don't listen to me. Penelope and I have been through the wringer and back again, but I do love her. Very much. I'm just jet-lagged, and an old lady."

"You're not old."

"Of course not," she says. "I'm thirty-five."

The doorbell rings then, and I lift myself out of the chair, but Irina waves me off.

"I'll get it."

She pads out of the kitchen and down the hallway to the front door. I hear a woman's voice on the other side.

I take my phone out of my bag. A missed call from my mom, a text from Kendra confirming the plan to see the new Marvel movie at a screening this weekend, and one from Jake. It's a linked article: "Tracking the History of the Carburetor."

It immediately makes me smile. And then I read it. Turns out the last carburetor was used in 1994.

I get it, now. You're McFly.

A moment later my phone pings: High-level response. And then a second: What are you doing tonight?

At my boss's.

It's almost seven!

I'm off the clock. We're just hanging.

I see the bubbles appear and disappear, appear and disappear, then: Up for a drink after?

We meet at Zinqué, a restaurant on Melrose with mediocre food but great atmosphere. Jake orders us both tequila and lime and we settle into a two-top in the corner. He's wearing a white long-sleeved waffle-knit Henley and dark jeans, and the ends of his hair are still wet from the shower. He smells good, too.

"What did you do tonight?" I ask him.

"I participated in a fantasy draft." He makes a *Yikes* face. "Feel free to show yourself out."

"I used to play soccer when I was younger," I say.

Jake's face lights up. "Me too! I sometimes still play in this league here. It's coed, if you ever want to come."

I shake my head. "Oh, no. Exercise isn't really a part of my adult life, what with all the sweating, and the fact that I now have a hair-care regimen. But that sounds fun."

Jake's eyes graze over me. "I find that hard to believe."

I pick up a strand of hair. "OK, fine, it's not a regimen—it's more like I use conditioner now, but still."

Jake smiles and shakes his head. "Not what I mean."

I hold his gaze. "I know."

Our drinks come. I squeeze the lime on the ridge into the drink and drop it inside.

"So you and your boss are buddies?" Jake asks.

"I wouldn't say buddies, exactly. But, yes, I do like her. And I don't often turn down free Thai food."

Jake nods twice in rapid succession. "Free Thai food. Noted."

"She's cool; she's extremely talented. She produces like twenty movies a year. I respect the hustle."

"Is that what you want someday?"

I'm not sure what to say. *No, not really, I don't have that kind of drive?* Or: *I still, at thirty-three, am not entirely sure what I want to do with my life.*

"I think I'm kind of a commitment-phobe."

Jake clears his throat. "Say more."

I put my elbows on the table. It's wood, unrefined. Lots of black hardware.

"I got kind of stuck after college, and, truthfully, sometimes I still am. It's not that I don't like my job, I do. I enjoy movies, I like assisting—I honestly think I'm good at it. But I don't know if I want Irina's job. I guess the most honest answer would be that I don't think I can have it."

I see Jake's eyes searching mine. "Why?"

"I feel like I missed the chance, maybe? I waited too long? Everyone I know who is on a stratospheric trajectory identified the steps a long time ago."

"I don't think that's true," Jake says. "You hear all the time about people getting their first acting job at fifty, directing their first movie at sixty, going back to medical school in their forties."

"When was the last time you heard about someone going to medical school in their forties?"

Jake sips, swallows. "I read about it. My point is it happens, all the time. There isn't just one way to achieve things. You can always be the exception."

I am the exception. I am the exception in so many ways—the anomaly, the point at which the sequencing blinked. I have something no one else does. Or, at least, to my knowledge no one else does. It feels selfish, maybe, to think I could be extraordinary in other areas, too. Maybe even dangerous—tempting fate just a little too far.

"You have to really want it," I say.

Jake looks at me, and I see it, what he means. Depth. The willingness to journey down, right to the center.

"Do you?" he asks.

His face is open, his shirt is unbuttoned at the collar. He looks like a door I could walk right through. And I want to. I want to let myself in. I want to tell him, this new place, all the things he does not yet know.

But it isn't time. We are just beginning. The big, deep questions I cannot get into. They are locked in a box under my bed. Sheets and sheets of paper.

Chapter Nineteen

I woke up in Big Sur and rolled over, reaching for Hugo. All I was met with was blank space. I sat up and looked outside—it was barely light out, the room was still half in shadow, the sun making a lazy debut. "Hugo?"

No answer.

I was naked underneath the covers, and I closed my eyes, replaying the images of the previous night—Hugo's mouth on my neck, his hands beside me, at my hips. The thick, heady sound of his voice.

There was a bathrobe slung over the chair by the bed, discarded from the night before, and I looped it around me, threading my hands through the arms and tying the knot.

Where was he?

I swung my feet over the bed, slid into slippers, and walked out onto our terrace.

The forest surrounding us was still sleeping. No sounds of

traffic or voices or electronics—there was even a visual silence. I could not see a single light or building, with the exception of the two bungalows in eyesight. Everything was pristine, untouched by all the color and sound of modern life. Below me, the ocean inhaled and exhaled in long, languid breaths.

When I was young, my parents would take me to Manhattan Beach. We'd park our car high up, to avoid parking lot fees, and then walk down the steep streets to the beach boardwalk. Sometimes we'd bring bikes, but mostly we set up shop in the sand: towels, a big umbrella, and a cooler full of food. My mother would always let me help her pack, so I knew in addition to rye bread and cheese there would be Goldfish and chocolate chip cookies. My father would go for a run in the sand, my mother always brought a book, and I'd haul back and forth between the ocean and her, screaming, running—salty and free.

The ocean was alive, then. I remember thinking if I just swam out far enough I could reach the crease where the water meets the sky. I could touch the horizon, run my hand along it's smooth edge.

Looking down at the ocean in Big Sur I wondered when that belief faded. Was it in a classroom, learning the world is round? But I have no memory of an aha moment, no recollection of any specific revelation. When do we stop believing in the things we do? And why does it happen so slowly instead of all at once?

It was cold out on the balcony. Probably close to forty degrees. I pulled the robe tighter around me and stuffed my hands down in the pockets. I could feel myself waking up, coming to life with every hazy, visual breath. One month. That was all it took. Four weeks to know that I wasn't going to listen. That no matter what that paper said, it wouldn't matter. I wanted him. I wanted to wake up with him and go to sleep with him. I wanted to stand behind him in the bathroom mirror in the morning, my face pressed against his wet back, as he got ready for work. I wanted his feet to find mine in the middle of the night. I wanted to be his first phone call, the place he rested from the chaos of the rest of the world, the constant friction of the pace of his life. I wanted to be *it* for him. I wanted so much more than ninety days. I wanted everything.

"Good morning."

I turned to see Hugo making his way toward me. He was wearing his running clothes and carrying two coffees. He sipped from one, and then set them down on the side table and wrapped his arms around me. I leaned my head into his chest. He was damp from his workout, and he smelled like our surroundings—sweaty and earthen.

I reached up and ran my fingers through his hair. His eyes looked into mine.

"Hey," he said. "How did you sleep?"

But I just shook my head. I moved my hands to his face and then reached up, balancing on tiptoes, and kissed him.

His mouth tasted like coffee, and I pulled him down—wanting him closer, tighter in.

Hugo's hands found the tie of my robe, and then they were untangling me, letting the terry cloth fall open. When his fingers landed on my body, they were cold, and I reacted back, but it took no more than a split second for my skin to adjust to his temperature. His fingers drew strokes against my abdomen—up and down.

I pulled him inside.

We tore at each other. Clothes, running shoes, the rest of the robe. I sat back in bed, and he leaned over me, breathing hard.

"You are so sexy," he said. He didn't let the words run. *So. Sexy.* "Tell me what you want." His voice was ragged, hazy, like the morning around us.

"I want you."

He leaned down and put his lips on mine. He held his body against me so there was no space between us. I felt the weight of him—his significance—all six feet two inches. "I'm right here," he said.

And then he was pressing into me. I closed my eyes and then opened them, and saw him looking back at me. There were beads of sweat on his forehead, his shoulders worked in tandem, rolling toward me, I reached up and grabbed onto his biceps.

I was, all at once, struck by two opposing feelings. The desire to stay that way forever, to never break apart, to spend my whole life in that state of intimate ecstasy. And then: to experience that release. The pleasure of certainty, of knowing that what was coming, had.

I felt that fire building in me. It started in my belly and radiated out to my limbs, fingers, feet, and toes, until I was engulfed in flames.

"Hugo," I said. He moved in answer—under me, over me, inside me. Everywhere, all at once.

"Tell me," he said, right into my ear. *Tell me tell me tell me.*

Chapter Twenty

Sorry," Jake says. "The breaker on the hall light is out. Here." I feel Jake's hand grab mine as we walk in darkness through his front door and then the click of a switch, and light.

His apartment is the same as it was the other night—but a little bit tidier—the blanket on the couch is folded with no corners showing, there are no errant glasses on the table.

"Can I get you something to drink?" Jake asks.

"Just water," I say.

"Coming right up."

He disappears into the kitchen, and I sit down on the couch. The night is foggy, and the darkness outside feels blanketing, heavy. Or maybe it's just that I've finally stopped moving.

Jake hands me a glass and settles down next to me. "It's tap," he says. "My Brita broke."

"I don't believe in Britas," I tell him. "I think they are a scam."

He squints. "You're probably right."

I take a sip and set it down on the coffee table. Jake puts a hand on my knee and then threads his fingers through mine. I feel the warmth of his hand, the warmth of him. And then I feel something else—some other force creep in between us. Expectation, maybe. The knowledge that what happens now matters in a way it never has before. All the things I know that he doesn't.

"Jake," I say.

"Yeah."

"There's something I have to tell you."

He sits back until he's looking at me, but he doesn't release my hand. I feel his thumb run over my knuckles.

"What's up?"

"I'm not—" I say. "I'm not exactly like other women."

Jake laughs. "I'm well aware of that," he says. "And I very much like it."

I shake my head. "The thing is—" I take a breath, figuring out what to say. How do I tell him that I know something that will change his life irrevocably? How do I share something this unbelievable?

"It's OK," Jake says. "You don't have to do anything you're not ready to do."

And then I feel it—all at once, like a whirlpool in my stomach. The pull of my attraction for him. It's shows up spontaneously, like a genie in a cloud of smoke. Poof.

"No," I say. "I want to."

Jake puts a hand on my face, and then we are kissing. In seconds I'm on top of him, my knees on either side of his stomach, my mouth on his neck, my hands in his hair, on his shoulders, grasping for anything I can reach.

His hands work down my back to my waist. Our mouths do battle—like we're trying to find something in each other, some hidden key buried under teeth and gums and bone.

He sits up further, his hands cupping my shoulders, and then he kisses my ear. "Do you want to go to my bedroom?" he asks. His voice is ragged, but it breaks at the end—the comedy sneaking in.

"Yes," I say.

He stands up and takes my hand and leads me back. I inhale and exhale slowly as we walk. I've never been in his bedroom before. White walls and a blue comforter. There are framed photos on his nightstand and dresser. He's behind me, his hands on my waist. I pick up a photo.

"Who's this?" I ask.

There's a tiny blond child, a girl, all ringlets, smiling as she hangs over a goldendoodle puppy.

"Maya," he says. His lips land on my earlobe. "I'll tell you later."

"Your sister's kid?"

Jake stops, exhales. "Yeah. She's sunshine."

"She looks it."

"I love her so much," he says. "I honestly can't believe how fast she is growing up. It's crazy. It's like a miracle or something."

There is no posturing with Jake. He is so pure—everything he says, he means.

Jake whispers into my ear. "Do you want children?"

I have not spent a lot of time thinking about kids. I had no idea how they would fit into this equation. But that doesn't seem like the right answer here. I'm not even sure it's true anymore.

There's something about Jake that makes me want to be honest. Maybe the truth is I don't know what I really want. Maybe it's changing.

"Not tonight," I say.

He smiles and moves his hands to my back. I loop my arms around his neck and then we are locked back together. We fall onto the bed, and Jake scrambles to get the pillows off.

"Someone explain decorative pillows to me," he says.

"No one knows, everyone just has them."

"We need to start asking ourselves why." He takes a silk blue-and-brown-striped one and tosses it dramatically to the foot of the bed, then turns back to me.

"Sorry," he says. "Where were we."

I get up and turn off the light. And then I lean back over him in the darkness. I walk my fingers up his chest and pull down on the collar of his shirt. "Here," I say.

He threads his hand through my hair and brings my lips down to his. His kisses are incredible. Soft and seeking and increasingly urgent. Like the quiet roar of a tidal wave. All of a sudden, I feel like we're about to be swept underneath the surface.

Our clothes come off quickly.

And then he's lying on top of me naked. It's quiet in the room. I can hear my breathing.

Jake gets a condom from the nightstand, and then he's back, kissing my neck, his hands tracing my belly.

"Is this OK?" he asks.

I move underneath him in answer.

I do not believe sex is a marker of anything but what you assign to it. It does not measure the seriousness of a relationship, is not a barometer for the amount of feeling, and has little to do with love, at least in causation. But lying underneath Jake I wonder if sex might express something else—some level of tenderness. If we might be able to judge not the strength of a person's feelings but the measure of their care.

Chapter Twenty-One

"So, how was it?"

Hugo and I are at brunch at Toast, a trendy eatery on Third Street in West Hollywood that Hugo loves and I think is fine.

"How did you even know?"

Hugo laughs. "Do you really want me to answer that?"

I take my sunglasses off and stare at him. "Because we were once in bed together?"

Hugo grins. He picks up his coffee. "I talk to you about what's going on in my life, I just want you to feel free to have the same privileges."

"You're so generous."

"I know," he says. "I'm going to buy you breakfast, too."

I take another sip of coffee. Hugo looks at me thoughtfully.

"But seriously, Daph. What's the deal?"

The deal is that I spent the night with Jake; he woke me up

with coffee and immediately asked if he could see me the following night. The deal is that he texts me throughout the day, asking how I'm doing and sending funny memes or jokes. The deal is that he might be the best person I've ever dated.

"I like him," I say. "I really like him. He's thoughtful and sincere. I've never met a person who just says what he means like that."

Hugo runs a hand over the bottom of his face. "Yeah," he says. "Admirable."

"That's actually a really great way to describe him."

"So you're having admirable sex."

I laugh. "'Thoughtful sex' maybe is better."

Hugo considers this. "Can I ask you something?"

"Yes," I say. "You were thoughtful. It's just different."

Hugo shakes his head. "No. I'm just wondering if you ever really saw me as someone you could be with."

I feel my shoulders tighten. I roll my neck from side to side. "What do you mean?"

Hugo sticks a hand back on his chin and massages the skin there. He doesn't look at me. "I just mean, was there ever a point where you thought, I don't know, it could go longer than three months?"

We never talk about this. What happened happened. We became friends. Our friendship is predicated on treading lightly on the past and staying firmly in the present.

"Hugo," I say. "You know this already. Our paper said three months."

"Right," he says. "Of course." But his tone sounds bitter all of a sudden, even a little angry around the edges.

"What's with you? Did you and Natalie break up or something?"

"No," he says. "No, I mean, I don't know. We can't break up—we're not together."

"Right," I say. "Then what?"

He turns his gaze back to me, dead center. "I think about it," he says. "Sometimes. I know I'm not supposed to say that, but I do."

I inhale slightly. I can feel the sweat on my back. It's a hot day, and there doesn't seem to be any air-conditioning in here. My cotton T-shirt is suctioned to me like Saran Wrap.

"You don't," I say. "Not really. You just think you do because I'm with someone now and we're talking about it."

"Don't say that," he says. "I hate being a cliché."

"It's true. Hugo, we've been broken up for five years. You have never once wished for things to be different."

Hugo shakes his head. "How do you know?"

I think about how Hugo and I became friends, after our breakup. How it felt seamless, almost—like he was meant to be in my life. I liked that I didn't have to lose him like I had everyone else. I didn't think I could bear to, honestly.

We met for coffee, a month after, and then ran into each other in line at Erewhon three weeks after that. Hugo suggested lunch, and then we just started spending time together.

One lunch turned into five years. Five years of drunken nights and hungover mornings and girlfriends and boyfriends and birthday parties and New Year's Eves at midnight. There have been times I've thought about it—of course I have. But my time with Hugo was up. We never backslid.

"Hugo, come on."

He shakes his head and picks up his water glass. "You're right. Maybe I'm more fucked up about Natalie than I think I am."

I feel something sharp pinch my stomach and then a deflation. Disappointment and relief, all in one. Because Hugo doesn't miss me. He's just having some crisis of identity, and I'm the closest thing he has to a therapist right now.

"Listen," I say. "Maybe you want a relationship."

Hugo laughs. "Ha. Right. Home sweet home."

"I'm serious. When was the last time you've even been monogamous?"

He peers at me, and I swallow, because of course. It was five years ago.

"So have you told him?" Hugo asks.

I glance down at my plate—a half-eaten bagel with scallion cream cheese, tomatoes, and capers—and then back up at him. "No," I say.

Hugo nods. "I guess I'm still special, then."

I raise my eyebrows at him, and he looks back at me. But he does not appear triumphant. There is something even sad about the way he says what he does next: "I'm still the only one who knows your secret."

Chapter Twenty-Two

Three months go by, and then two more. Jake and I keep seeing each other. Our relationship progresses slowly and easily—like an open road with no traffic. We just keep moving forward.

I start spending the night regularly, and then entire weekends dissolve in his apartment—pizza boxes and old movie rentals. I bring Murphy. He and Saber get along like Craigslist roommates. They don't go out of their way to engage, but they don't seem to have a problem with each other, either.

Jake gets me an electric toothbrush. The whole thing—its own base and cord.

And then, in late winter, Jake asks me if I'd like to move in with him.

He is sitting on the couch, and I'm on the floor, a box of SUGARFISH sushi on the coffee table in front of us—tuna and cucumber rolls and salmon sashimi—when he just out and says it.

"Do you want to live here?"

I pick up a roll with my chopsticks. "What do you mean?"

"I mean, do you want to move in with me and have this be your home, too?" He dunks a piece of salmon into the soy sauce. "Could save on toilet paper and apples. I buy a lot of apples."

I put down my chopsticks and arch around to look at him. He is smiling—a big, goofy grin.

"You're serious?"

"I am," he says. "I've been thinking about it a lot lately. You're here all the time, and I think we like being together." He peers at me. "We do, right? The place is big enough for us, and Murphy and Saber."

It's true—in the last six weeks I've spent more time in Wilshire Corridor than I have in West Hollywood. I've even become friends with Jake's neighbors, Mrs. Madden especially. She bakes me almond crescent cookies for Shabbat. Every Friday there's a tin outside Jake's door.

"Of course we do. I love being here."

But I also love my place. It's funky and likely molding. There are cracks in the kitchen floor and peeling paint in the closets. But it's been my home for seven years. I know all the corners, the way the floor bows in the bedroom by the dresser, and how the bathroom tiles always get loose and you have to put them back like puzzle pieces. I have no idea if I'm ready to give it up.

"Is that a yes?"

"That's a big step."

Jake nods slowly. "I know. I'm not scared of it, though. Feels right to me."

I turn back to our sushi. In the past five months we have gotten to know each other in small and big ways—areas I've never crossed into with anyone else. Jake has met my family, and seen me hangry and knows, now, I need to get my hair colored every three weeks otherwise I have a ton of premature gray. But he does not know the thing I keep trying to tell him. He does not know about the pieces of paper, what they mean.

I feel Jake's hands on my shoulders. He begins to knead them, and as soon as he does I can feel the tension leaving my body. I feel the way I always do around him—calm and good.

"This is a lot at once, I know," he says. "Especially for the commitment-phobe." I can hear the play in his voice, that easy chuckle that is so very Jake.

"Not anymore."

He smiles. He cups my shoulder with his palm. "All I'm asking is that you think about it."

I turn to face him, and he leans his lips down to meet mine. He tastes like pickled ginger and beer. Delicious.

"OK," I say. "I'll think about it."

"It would be fun," he says. "We could stay up late and eat tons of sugar."

"We're not twelve."

"We're not?" He clears his throat. "Well, that explains the sex."

He puts both of his hands on either side of my rib cage. I peel away in laughter.

"It would just be nice," he says. He holds me gently, now. "Murphy likes it here, too."

"Murphy is afraid of heights," I say. "He still hasn't made up his mind."

"We'll work it out. I'll put up a silk screen of a dog park." He pauses. "I want you to be here."

I kiss him. "I want to be here, too."

I think about all that intimacy, the impossibility of secrets. How do you hide anything in eight hundred square feet?

"You don't," Kendra says when I tell her. We are in Irina's kitchen the following night. Kendra is perched on a counter stool, nursing a Starbucks mint tea, and I'm going through Irina's mail.

"I love my place. You know that."

Kendra shrugs. "Change is the only constant in life, babe. Bless it. You had five great years there."

"Seven."

"Even better. Jake is an amazing guy, and he cares about you, and he wants to make a life with you. And I think you feel that way, too. Things could be a lot worse."

"I know," I say. "Obviously. But isn't it a little bit soon? We haven't even been dating for half a year."

"When it's right you just know," Kendra says. "Joel and I got married after six weeks."

"That was an unusual situation."

"Yeah, only in that it took me four days to go from hating the idea of marriage to not being able to conceive of my life without him."

"I don't know," I say. "I like the idea of marriage."

I think about Jake—the safety and calm I get at being in his presence. But I've spent my life knowing everything would end. That nothing was forever. It's hard to transition to the inverse.

"You're not me," Kendra says. She picks her cup up and sips. "Love is not only one thing, you know. Love is just the thing you need. For me it was an instant change of heart. For you it's something else."

I drop some junk mail into the trash. "How romantic."

Kendra rolls her eyes. "Give me a break," she says. "What do you want to do? Play cat and mouse with someone like Hugo forever?"

As soon as she says it I feel immediately sad. Hugo and I have seen less of each other lately. He's been traveling a ton, always on the weekends, and I've been at Wilshire Corridor more nights than I'm not. Last Saturday Jake and I ordered Pizzana, watched some *Bachelorette* knockoff, and fell asleep before ten.

There's a warmth to this relationship with Jake, a comfort that I've never really felt or known before. But sometimes I'm afraid it means I'm somehow fading—that all the bright and brilliant aspects of myself are diminishing in this cocoon. That I will not have the sparkle I once had—that all my edges are being worn down in this intimacy.

"Obviously not," I say.

"What are we discussing?" Irina appears in the kitchen, a Bluetooth headpiece in her ear, and her cell phone in another. She's wearing leather pants and a tight black turtleneck, even though it's unseasonably warm for February.

"Are you talking to us?" Kendra asks in a low voice.

"Of course!" Irina snaps. She looks at Kendra. "You are here too often. Don't you have a new job?"

"I do; I just miss you," Kendra says. She smiles, and Irina pats her playfully on the back. "We're remote half-time anyway, now."

"Yes," Irina says. Her tone is deadpan. "You seem hard at work."

"We're discussing the fact that Jake asked Daphne to move in with him."

Irina whirls to face me. "You're kidding."

"Oh, wow, thanks. I feel so cherished here."

Irina shoots me a look. "That's not what I meant, and you know it. Don't be obvious."

"It's soon," I say. "Living together is a big step."

"A giant one," she says. "Make sure you feel the same way about nontoxic cleaning products and how to get rid of squirrels."

"Specific," Kendra says.

"I'm more worried about that kind of access," I say.

Irina looks at me. "His to you or yours to him?"

"There are things he doesn't know."

"Like what?" Kendra says. "That sometimes you don't recycle? Who cares?"

Irina comes over and touches my arm. She's rarely this affectionate, but when she is, I know how much she means it. "You do what you're comfortable with, baby. And if you move in and you don't like it, move out. You can always change it. And change it again. And again. The stakes do not have to be that high."

"Isn't that a Tony Robbins saying?" Kendra asks. "If something isn't working, change it. Keep changing it until it works?"

"It's a Penelope saying," she says, somewhat wearily. "So, honestly, probably."

"I'm just not sure what's stopping you," Kendra says. And then she squints at me. "Unless I am."

I wave her off. "I've never lived with a guy before."

"But he's Jake," Kendra says. "He's like the best one."

I smile. "He is."

"So, problem solved."

I get home to my apartment a little after nine. I drop my sweater on the couch and pad into the bedroom. I sit down on the floor and reach under the bed. My fingers find it quickly. It's not big, maybe two feet by two feet—a box. My box. Filled with paper. There are postcards and fortunes from inside cookies, and the corner of a rolled-up newspaper.

Peter, five weeks.

Josh, six months.

Stuart, one night.

They mark out my life in units of time. Days, weeks, months, years. I take the last piece of paper out of my bag, the one I've been carrying around since I met Jake, five months ago, now.

I place it inside.

Chapter Twenty-Three

Tae, two years and two months.

Tae and I met my junior year of college, on a boat in the middle of the Pacific Ocean. We had both signed up for this orientation-at-sea thing, where you sailed out to Catalina Island, off the coast of Southern California, and spent the day there. It was part of a marine biology prerequisite, which I definitely was not majoring in, but it seemed like a nice excuse to get off campus.

Tae was not impressed. He was premed, barreling toward Stanford medical school, and did not have time for any unfocused hours on the ocean.

When I first encountered him, he was arguing with the TA on the boat. "I thought this was a biology dive. Do you mean to tell me we're sailing to Catalina for *recreation?*" He made the word sound dirty.

The TA, her name was Kensington—I remember because

everyone called her Kenny, like the *South Park* character—told Tae that the trip was educational in nature and necessary to pass the pre-req biology class, which he was taking.

Tae grumbled into a life jacket.

There were maybe twelve students on the boat, all in. While everyone gathered inside and toward the back to add vodka from their book bags into their lemonade, I sat in the front. Boats always make me nauseous—something I'd forgotten.

Tae came up to me and held out a towel. "This seat taken?"

I gestured next to me; he spread the towel, and sat.

"Pinch the spot between your thumb and forefinger," he said, without looking at me.

"What?"

"You're seasick; it helps." He gestured to me with his own hand. I tried on mine.

"Here," he said. He took my hand in his and pressed down on the pad of my thumb. There was a sensation of sharp pain, like a spasm, and then I felt the pressure shift slightly out of my abdomen.

"That actually works."

"Indeed," he said, still holding my hand. He kept his thumb pressed on mine, more or less, until we got to the island.

Tae was direct. He'd grown up in a home with immigrant parents, who were both doctors themselves. He didn't have a lot of time for conjecture, or frivolity. He loved science—the cold, hard facts of life. He was passionate about the environment—encouraging me to recycle, refusing to get coffee to go, unless he had his stainless steel cup. I drew the line at composting in my campus apartment—or my roommate did.

"This isn't a commune," she'd said when Tae brought over a plastic bin and chucked a banana peel inside.

He was witty, too. His exacting nature translated to his thoughts. And he was dazzlingly handsome—tall, lean, with just the right amount of musculature and a face that was so symmetrical I used to joke with him that he came out of a test tube. His physical perfections would have been grating if it weren't offset by his severity, his humor, his beautiful and dogmatic way of looking at the world.

After the Catalina trip we began hanging out, as friends, at the medical school library. Tae lived in a shitty student house that was basically a stone's throw from his classes. If I wanted to find Tae, I knew where to look. He was either at the grad library, or in the lab. And if neither of those were true, he was home, sleeping.

I liked school—I liked the structure of it; I thrived off the predictable rhythm and pace. The energy. I also loved that I could schedule classes only after 11:00 a.m.

The medical school had the best rooms for quiet study—the library was always crowded and too loud, despite the silence rule. There was just too much foot traffic, too many students who came and went frequently. But in the medical school, if you were studying, you were studying for *hours.*

It was the following weekend, Friday night. It was sorority and fraternity rush—the week all the houses on campus picked their new recruits for the year. Very few medical students entered the Greek system—there just wasn't enough time—but still, the library was less than at capacity.

I asked Tae a question about our course. I wasn't understanding genetic engineering.

"What is a vector used for?" I whispered to Tae.

He thumbed his notebook and then handed it to me. *A vector is used to transfer genetic material into a host organism.*

I copied some notes down, and studied a bullet-pointed infographic at the bottom of the page.

And that's when I felt it. Like a fire, right across my chest.

I remember Tae turning to me, at first annoyed, maybe, that some sudden movement or sound had interrupted his flow. Then his face changed to one of concern and then something else, something I'd rarely if ever seen directed at me, not since I'd fallen off the monkey bars and broke my arm in the second grade. Fear.

The pain didn't move, but it spread, and then it began to feel like I was suffocating, like I could not possibly figure out how to take a next breath. Tae called an ambulance. They gave me CPR in the back. They used a defibrillator. In three minutes, we were at the hospital.

They ran a lot of tests. At some point my parents showed up. I lost consciousness or was put under and then woke, and when I did, there was a team of doctors gathered in my room. I remember thinking it looked like a television show—the mix of color-coded scrubs, my father with his coffee, my mother in her glasses. Tae now somehow caught in our family drama. They couldn't have staged it better.

And that was when they told me. The thing I must now share. The truth I've been avoiding. There is not just one box under my bed, there are two. One measures my life in names and units of time, the other in milligrams.

This is a box filled with prescription notes, with complex words like *nitroglycerin* and *captopril* scrawled underneath a hospital insignia. There are bottles of aspirin, cholesterol medication, and diuretics, which help rid the body of sodium and water. There are lifestyle recommendations, the limits of my physical activity, no salt. There are logs of hospital stays and procedures. I even have a different name, here. In this box I am the Patient.

The truth is hard. It's complicated. It does not always follow a simple structure. It is not always convenient. That's why sometimes we do our best to leave it out of the story for as long as possible. We choose to let it linger in the corners, we don't spotlight it. But eventually, it catches up to us. Of course it does.

You can run but you can't hide.

Chapter Twenty-Four

The doctors use complicated medical jargon, words and phrases it will take me weeks to properly understand or pronounce. They tell me I have what's called congenital heart disease, which I learn is really a catch-all for *something is seriously wrong with your heart.* It's been there since birth but undetected until now. They tell me I had an SCA or a sudden cardiac arrest. They tell me it's not a heart attack—it's actually much worse. My heart stopped beating. It's a miracle I survived, few ever do.

Then they get around to it—after the caveats and the complicated phrasing—they tell me my heart is failing.

"*Why?*" my mother asks.

I am a runner, I'm twenty-one years old. I have a full social life. I party a lot and I sleep little. How can my heart be failing? It's barely even begun.

A genetic defect. No one knows why or how it happened. Neither of my parents have it, they test them.

"An anomaly," the doctors say. Unexplainable.

From in my bed, the machines beeping, I let out a laugh. Because of course. What, did I think there was no reason? Did I think the universe didn't want something from me in return?

I have information you don't, I thought often. From that hospital room I could almost hear the cosmic whisper: *So do I.*

They told me they'd categorize my whole situation as stage two. They did not immediately tell me how many numbers there were. It will get worse, maybe even quickly, no one knows when, but it can move in only one direction. If you get to four (the final, I found out) sometimes patients need a heart transplant—but that was no picnic and these doctors, they wanted me to know that. Patients didn't always make the list, the older and sicker they got, the harder it was, sometimes their bodies rejected the hearts, the anti-rejection medications could cause cancer—the problems went on.

My mother began to cry, my father looked like he could not remember where he'd left his keys.

Their words sounded like an avalanche—they just kept falling, burying the life I had known, had thought I knew, was maybe even planning. Limited activity, lifestyle modifications, medications, surgeries. Likely no pregnancy. The lists of all the ways in which my life would not look like everyone else's. All the ways I now had to hold my breath, to prepare, to inhale and inhale and inhale only.

From twenty-one to twenty-three I was in and out of the hospital. I began a cocktail of medications—trial and error and error again. There were procedures, surgeries. I had an ICD pacemaker inserted. I stopped playing soccer.

Tae stayed with me through it all—until we found some stability, some combination of milligrams and devices that worked, that has worked, up until now. We didn't break up because of my failing heart or the fact that I had to graduate remotely or the reality that Tae was in medical school in San Francisco. No, we broke up because of shitty cell service.

When I was in the hospital, Tae would come and study. He was concerned for me, but I also think he liked being in the trenches, so to speak. While other medical students were reading stories like mine in textbooks, Tae was in the hospital, getting to know the doctors, seeing things firsthand. He'd read my test results, sit in on meetings with the team. I was his lived education.

"You didn't call me," he said. It was a Friday. I'd been home for three weeks. We were in my bedroom, and Tae was spending the weekend with me. I remember thinking it felt almost normal. Just a twentysomething boyfriend and girlfriend trying to figure out how they were going to spend Saturday. At her parents' house, but still.

These last few months had been better. I was even thinking about getting an internship for the summer—trying to salvage what might remain of my postgraduate life, two years later. While my friends had moved on to shitty entry-level jobs climbing the corporate ladder, or grad school, or traveling the world, I'd been locked in a time warp that had brought me directly back to childhood—but with none of the play and all of the rules. At a moment where I was supposed to be experiencing so much independence—*congratulations, graduates*—I was now more reliant on my parents than I'd been since I was five years old. After surgery my mother fed me and often bathed me, my father ran my errands—the pharmacy, Macy's for a new neck pillow, battery replacements, ice cream. They tucked me in at night, sometimes my father would even read.

There had been so much going on the past two years that I had forgotten our end was coming, Tae's and mine. It was time for the universe to come collect.

"I called you," I said. "It was totally fine. Eisner said he doesn't even want to see me until next month."

Tae had asked me to call him from the hospital, like I always did.

"It didn't ring."

"My cell reception sucks there," I told him. "You know that."

It was true, too. It was true except for the fact that he was right: I hadn't called. I did not want to be sick that weekend. I wanted to be twenty-three. I wanted to call my boyfriend about whether he wanted mushrooms on his pizza, not what my echocardiogram said.

"What about Wi-Fi?" he asked.

I sat up. I was feeling good. I was wearing jeans.

"What's up with you tonight?"

From our first kiss—the week after my diagnosis, no less, Tae was now an intricate, central part of this unfolding new story—I'd relied on him. In ways that were obvious, in ways that were unfair. He'd held me sobbing on the bathroom floor, and my hand before surgery. He'd slept in hospital chairs, respectfully looked away when catheters and IV lines were inserted. He'd picked up my parents, bleary-eyed, at 2:00 a.m. from the emergency room entryway. He'd been there.

In the past two months, though, I'd begun to stand on my own two feet. The medications were working. Things were stabilizing.

I felt good, or as good as I could ever remember feeling. I'd lost two years of my life, and I was ready to rejoin the world.

I knew it would never be normal. I knew at some point my heart would give out on me again. I knew there would be inflection points, if I was lucky enough to survive them. I knew I'd always need to be tethered to something—a device, a hospital, a scan, a machine. I knew there were no outs. But I wanted this thing with my heart to be happening in the other room. I did not want it to be in the same bed with me anymore.

"I was worried about you," Tae said. "You can't just not fucking call me."

"I'm fine," I said. "You have to get that. I'm better."

"You're not better," he said. He was practically screaming. "You can't get better."

I looked at him, incredulous. "That's a fucked-up thing to say to me."

"No, it's not, it's the truth."

"It's not the truth anymore."

"Daphne, be reasonable. We know this. I know this."

I got up and stood a few feet from him with my arms crossed. I felt the anger pulsing through my veins. I felt voracious, wild. I felt powerful.

"I'm not your fucking patient; I'm your girlfriend," I said.

Tae narrowed his eyes at me. They flashed. I honestly thought he might punch the wall, that's how focused in rage he looked. And then he started to cry. I had never seen him break down. Not in any of our hospital stays, not in the cafeteria, not after visiting hours, when the nurses who snuck him in finally told him it was time to go. He put a hand over his face. He was standing in the doorway to my childhood bedroom, backlit by the afternoon sun.

"God damn it," he said.

I just stood there, anger and sadness washing over me in twin waves.

"Daphne," he said. His voice was devoid of its prior intensity. "I don't want you to be sick. But I don't know how to do this anymore. I'm not sure we can. You want to be free, and I can't help but be here. Be worried. I don't know how to do it differently. I don't know how to not make love and worry the same thing."

And then I remembered: our sheet of paper.

Tae, two years and two months.

I closed the space between us. I wrapped my arms around him. I stood on my tiptoes and hugged him, clutching on to his neck. We'd been physically intimate so much less than we should have been, I thought. So much less than we deserved to be.

"Thank you," I said.

He seemed confused, and then he wasn't; he couldn't be. He had seen me through what he needed to. He had been there for the impossible unfolding of it all, he had held the walls up when everything inside them was falling and breaking and crashing. *I don't know what I would have done without you* is such an overused phrase.

There was so much I didn't know. How long this hovering reality would last, whether I had anything to offer the world outside this home anymore. How I could possibly be with someone who didn't know—or maybe worse, who did. But I knew our time, Tae's and mine, was up. I was heartbroken, but I was also certain. What we had in common was my illness. And I could feel us both resenting that simple and constraining truth. I had fallen in love with the man who was there when my heart stopped. Now it was beating again, however cautiously, and we were reminders to each other of the worst of it. We always would be.

"I love you," he said.

"I love you, too."

When I did eventually get a new piece of paper—six months later—it felt like a promise. Like someone on the other end was seeing me, was seeing all of this, and still not counting me out. Every time after, I knew when I saw a name, when I saw that mark in days, weeks, months—that I would have that time, that it was now promised to me. I'd be alive. I'd get to live it.

I have a deal with the universe. I take my time in increments, and I get to stay here. For the time written, I get to keep my heart.

But now—

Now, I do not know anymore. A blank piece of paper should mean forever, right? But what if it just means I do not get to know? What if it now means anything could happen at any time? How do I reckon with an unknown that dangerous?

Chapter Twenty-Five

I have put this off for as long as possible but it's now nearly March and tonight, Hugo, Jake, and I are having dinner. Hugo is bringing a date—a girl named Claudia he started seeing a few weeks ago. Natalie ended sometime in the fall.

We're going to the Hotel Bel-Air, one of Hugo's favorite places in LA. I've already told Jake not to fight Hugo on the check—it's his thing; he won't relent. And I've explained to Hugo over the phone to try and just tone it down a little. Be cool.

"He's a nice guy," I tell Hugo. "And he's excited to meet you. Just be normal."

The truth is Hugo and I haven't seen a ton of each other since our brunch at Toast over five months ago. We've let our weekend ritual slide, and he's been out of town a lot. Jake and I have spent the night together at my place the last five consecutive Saturdays, so on Sundays we go to the farmers market together, now. They are always sold out of the sunflowers by the time we arrive.

I miss Hugo, though. I wonder if our friendship was predicated on us both being some degree of single. I know the caveat to men and women not being able to be friends is if one of them is in a relationship, but for us, I think it worked the opposite way. When we were alone we could fill in the other pieces. Now that Jake takes up so much of my life, where does Hugo fit into it?

The Hotel Bel-Air is tucked away in the hills of Los Angeles; it's an airy, stunning getaway for the rich and famous—or those with the private cell phone number of Denise, the manager. The restaurant is run by Wolfgang Puck, and it's excellent, too—situated in an open courtyard toward the back of the hotel—private booths to the side, the most beautiful bar, and white walls wrapped in ivy. It's a secluded, elite paradise that oddly isn't very celebrity populated. Unlike the Beverly Hills Hotel, there are never any paparazzi here.

Jake is wearing a blue cashmere sweater and dark jeans. He feels like a cloud when I tuck myself against him. I have black jeans and a sleeveless turtleneck on. I'm wearing a pair of strappy black heels that once again I know I'll have to take off by the end of the night.

Jake and I get there first, before Hugo and Claudia. He puts his arm around me. I lean my head into him.

"Are you nervous?" I ask his shoulder.

"Why?" he says. "Should I be?"

I tilt my head up to him. "No," I say. "I mean, I just would understand if you were."

"Because Hugo is so intimidating?"

"No, because he's important to me."

Jake lifts my chin up to his lips. He kisses me once. "Then I'm not nervous, I'm happy."

Hugo rounds the corner a moment later. He's alone, and jogging. He's wearing a black-and-blue-striped button-down, a black belt, and black pants. As soon as I see him, I realize how much I've missed his energy.

"Sorry," he says. "Sorry, I'm late."

He gives me a quick kiss on the cheek. And shakes Jake's hand. "Hey, man, hi. It's so nice to meet you."

Jake smiles; it feels genuine. "So nice to meet you, too. I was beginning to think you might not exist."

"I barely do these days," Hugo says. "I don't think I've spent three consecutive nights in LA in two months."

"Where's Claudia?" I ask.

Hugo waves me off as he moves toward the hostess desk. "She's not coming. Some mix-up with my personality. She decided she didn't like it. Hey, Gabrielle." He leans over and kisses the hostess on the cheek. "Can we have six?"

"Of course."

Gabrielle takes three menus and then leads us over to a booth toward the back right wall. It's tucked away—its own little oasis. "Enjoy."

Hugo sits, and then I let Jake slide in, so he's in the middle.

Hugo yanks at his collar. "It's hot today."

He's moving around like a caged bird, and he hasn't once made eye contact with me.

"Are you OK?"

"Fine," he says. He reaches for a water on the table and downs some. "Just one of those back-to-back days."

"You're right, it is hot," Jake says. He reaches behind and pulls his sweater up and over his head, before winking at me. My heart does a one-two step. The kindness of this man, his consideration—not for Hugo, but for me. He wants this night to go well, because I've told him it matters to me, and he's going out of his way to play diplomat.

"So," Hugo says. "Daph tells me that you work in Hollywood."

I feel my stomach tighten, one, because Hugo has just used my nickname—an unnecessary show of closeness—and two, because he makes *Hollywood* sound derogatory, even the word choice is dismissive.

But Jake does not blink. "Yes, I'm pretty lucky. I have a good gig and good bosses. For the most part, the people I work with are not too egomaniacal."

Hugo laughs. "That makes one of us."

"You're in real estate?"

"In theory," he says. "Mostly I talk people into doing things they don't want to do."

Jake smiles. "That would not be my strong suit."

The waitress appears again. We order drinks. A tequila and soda for Hugo, a beer for Jake, and a glass of red wine for me. I'm not supposed to drink a lot. Actually, I'm not really supposed to drink at all. It can interfere with my medication, it's inflammatory, a whole host of reasons why any vice could possibly be deadly. But there are only so many concessions I can make in this life, and alcohol isn't one of them.

"It's beautiful here," Jake says. He looks around.

"Have you ever been?"

Jake shakes his head.

"It's my sanctuary," Hugo says. "I come at least once a week. It's pricey, but worth it."

He's acting like an asshole, but also a nervous asshole. It's an interesting combo for Hugo, and not necessarily one I've seen before. I can tell, Jake can tell, and I can see Hugo can tell, too. That he wants to be difficult, like he's trying to win some invisible hand war. Elbows on the table.

I slip my hand into Jake's under the table. He squeezes back.

"I hear you guys are moving in together," Hugo says.

Jake looks over at me. "She hasn't exactly given me an answer."

Hugo downs more water. "Don't be tricky, Daph," he says.

"I'm not tricky," I say. "I'm just slow."

"Good luck getting her to get rid of any of her stuff," Hugo says.

Jake puts a hand around my shoulders. "It can all come. We'll make room. I love all your weird things."

Love. I still haven't told Jake—in fact, I haven't said it to a single man since Tae. Not because I didn't feel it—I felt it all the time. Love or not, I felt it with Josh in San Francisco, walking Marina Green at dusk. I felt it with Emil, during those six days I spent mostly in a loft downtown. I feel it with Jake when he puts toothpaste on my brush in the morning if he wakes up earlier than me, or hands me the remote after dinner.

And then there was Hugo.

But it always feels like the word is intrinsically tied to power, like I will be ceding mine by laying it down.

Jake told me he loved me two months ago, over Mexican at Pink Taco on the Sunset Strip. I had chicken fajitas, and Jake was eating fish tacos. A basket of chips and guacamole sat on the picnic table in between us. We were out on the patio, traffic speeding past.

I was telling Jake about work that day, and about this charcoal cleanse Irina was on. From what I could tell it involved drinking large volumes of charcoal dissolved in water, and an array of vitamins that took up half a bowl.

"Does she ever consult a licensed medical professional?" he asked me.

"Depends how you define *professional*," I told him. "And also perhaps what constitutes a 'license.'"

"Ideally something as official as what we use to drive."

"Oh," I said. "Most don't even have that. Carbon footprint, and all."

"So you're saying that in a weird way she's actually an environmentalist?"

I spooned some guacamole onto my plate. Chips have salt. I was counting them. "I'm saying that you could find the good in anyone."

Jake put down his seltzer. He looked at me from across the table so long without speaking that I knew what was coming next. I could feel it. The way you can tell it's going to rain.

"I love you," he said. So simply. He let it sit there, stretch out across the table, a whirl of dazzling, glittering words.

He kept smiling at me. But not in a way that made me feel

like he was waiting for my response. In fact, his smile got bigger with my silence, like just the act of saying it was his joy, like he'd been holding it inside—this display of sparkle—for longer than he could bear.

"You mean more to me than I know how to express right now," I said. Because it was true. It wasn't that I didn't love him. It was that there were things I had to tell him before I told him that.

Because the thing is, Jake doesn't know. He doesn't know I am sick. He knows only that there are two scars on my chest—a childhood surgery, I told him, the same lie I've told them all. Something old that is no longer relevant or active. My ICD, once noticeable, has hidden with age. Even the scar from the battery replacement surgery is easy to miss. My breasts cover it; it's simpler to skate around now. He knows that I do not run—I hate exercise, I say, shopping is my cardio. He knows that my medications—hidden, taken with care and discipline—are for my mental health. When I have to go to the doctors—for tests, weekly sometimes—only Irina and my parents are aware of my whereabouts.

Every time I've tried to tell him the truth, I pull back. *He doesn't deserve this.* And then: *He doesn't deserve me—he does not deserve everything that comes along with me.*

Jake has already lost someone. How can I tell him that someday he will lose me, too? I finally have a relationship that is not defined by time.

"I'm starving," I tell Hugo and Jake. "Let's order."

"They make a grilled halibut and a steak off-menu that are excellent," Hugo says. "Jake, do you eat red meat?"

Jake shrugs. "Sure, not often."

"I'm on keto these days." Hugo pats his stomach. "I need to be better about it."

"Keto?" Jake asks. "I've never heard of it."

Hugo gives me an incredulous stare. "You're kidding."

Jake looks to me and back. "Not up on diet culture, I guess."

I see Hugo react. The slight flare of his nostrils when he's pissed. "It's not really a diet."

Jake waves him off. "I didn't mean— Look, I pretty much eat anything."

Hugo looks back down at the menu. "Lucky you."

I feel the tension at the table. I pick up my water glass. "Where does everyone stand on cheese?" I ask.

"Solidly pro," Jake says.

"Sure," Hugo says. "You guys order. Whatever you want."

A couple walks by. The girl is in a short sundress and cardigan and black boots. I see Jake take a small notebook out of his back pocket and jot something down.

I look from the couple to him and back again.

"What's going on?" Hugo asks. "You a poet in your spare time?"

Jake shakes his head. "No, I have this thing."

"The boots!" I call out. A table next to us turns, and I lower my voice. "Any time Jake sees someone in Doc Martens he has to write it down. It's a superstition." I look to Jake. "Right?"

"More or less."

Hugo looks back down at the menu. "Huh." He turns to me. "Are you having the off-menu pomodoro or are you finally going to try something new?"

I don't look at him. "Haven't decided."

Hugo turns to Jake. "Don't believe her, man. She always orders the same thing." He looks back to me. "It's cute."

I see Jake clock it, and I brace myself. For him to punch back, which he has every right to. But instead he just says: "I love a woman who knows what she wants. I'll get your pomodoro, and you can have some. Pasta is always good."

I want to grab him and kiss him right there at the table.

As predicted, Hugo insists on paying. Jake tries to fight him on it but gives up quickly. We all walk the pathway out of the restaurant and over the archway above the pond to our cars.

Jake goes to hand in our valet slips, and I pull Hugo aside.

"You were cocky," I tell him.

"I was me." He pulls a twenty-dollar bill out of his wallet. "Nice guy."

"That's it?"

Hugo looks back at me. "He's a solid dude. I like him. He honestly seems like a great match for you."

And then Jake is back. He slips a hand around my waist, and we all hug goodbye—the warmest of partings. Jake promises to get Hugo the number of the rare-car dealer they used on a period piece last year. Hugo claps his back.

"Great to meet you, man," he says. "I'm sure I'll see you soon."

Once we're in the car, Jake puts a hand on my knee. "Great guy," he says.

"He acted like an asshole."

"Yeah," he says. "He did. But he's high energy. He seems like he'd be fun."

I shake my head. "You really could find a redeeming quality in anyone."

Jake pauses, thoughtful. Then: "I feel for him, Daphne," he says. He's silent for a moment. "It's not his fault he's still in love with you."

Chapter Twenty-Six

Hugo and I had been dating for two months and three weeks when I was rushed to the hospital. I had been counting down the days, even hours. I could see the blinking marker of three months, like a skull-and-bones warning of a rocky cliff below. DANGER. I didn't know how to paddle backward. I didn't know how to stop us from free-falling over.

I was in love with him. That was God's honest truth. Everything about our relationship felt big and epic and heady. I loved the way his brain worked. How he was always trying to play devil's advocate—to see and appreciate sides that were not his own. And I loved how stubborn he was—steadfast. His confidence sometimes felt like a bulldozer, but other times it felt like a foundation—like I was tethered to something that could not possibly bend or snap or break. His personality made me feel safe, being in his orbit was like being inside the sun—the rays couldn't harm me, all I felt was the warmth of proximity.

I didn't want it to end.

I was at Irina's when I felt the terrifying sensation. Irina called 911 on the spot.

"She has a heart condition," she said to the EMTs.

She'd found out almost at the start of when I began working for her. It's true what Irina says: it's impossible to hide anything from her. I am grateful for her discretion all these years. She has never made me feel anything less than capable, and she has always looked out for me.

I was rushed to the ER. A process I knew too well. It's strange, in all the years I've been at this, in all the hospital stays and procedures and scary surgeries, I never believed I might die. It was foolish not to—I should have. Everyone else did. And I knew, intellectually, maybe, that it could come, that maybe it was coming. But I never felt like it was now. I never believed in my real, tangible mortality. At least, until then.

I'm going to die, I thought. *This is how my relationship with Hugo ends.*

It seemed so clear. I did not know why I hadn't thought of it sooner. We were so deep in. Of course, finally. The obvious.

It turned out, I had stenosis in an artery. Which means one of my arteries was too narrow to properly pump blood.

"This is solvable, Daphne," Dr. Frank said, a phrase I had heard seldom if at all. "But with you and your history, it carries more risk than we'd like. And I don't love what it's signifying to us."

It meant something was progressing. It meant all was not well under the surface.

"We can put a stent in," he said. "We can go through your

groin, so open-heart is not necessary. This is a simple procedure, usually, but less simple with you." He nodded at me. Dr. Frank was direct; I liked that about him. He didn't treat me like a child. "Normally patients leave the same day, but we'll have to hang on to you. We should act quickly. Have you been feeling more tired? Any swelling?"

I thought about it. I had, lately, been feeling like I was moving through quicksand. But I often felt that way. It was hard for me to determine what feeling good was. It had been so long—nearly a decade now—that I had experienced anything I might compare to radiant health.

"I don't know," I said. "Maybe."

Dr. Frank grunted.

"How bad is this?" I asked him.

"Normally I'd tell a patient getting a stent that they had a less than one percent chance of death." He took a breath. "With you," he said, "it's different."

I know I am the patient, but sometimes in the hospital I can forget, we all can. We are a team, we are making decisions, analyzing data, collecting intel. I am a member of that team. My heart is a whiteboard, with lists and surveys scrawled on it. Sometimes I forget it's inside my body.

My parents came to the hospital. They dropped Murphy off at Wagville—one less thing to worry about. We scheduled the procedure for the next day.

I have a team of doctors—cardiologists and pulmonary experts and a psychologist. Everyone has a role. The team agreed with Dr. Frank—we'd act quickly.

Dr. Lisa, my pulmonary doctor, likes to refer to my heart as an ecosystem—like it has plants and fruits and birds and trees all its own. Like it's raining in there, keeping all sorts of tiny creatures hydrated and sustained. Except it isn't, of course. That's the problem.

When my parents went downstairs to get coffee, after the path forward had been clearly marked, I picked up my phone. I had four missed calls from Hugo, one voice mail, and a slew of text messages beginning with Want to have lunch? to Daphne, I'm worried. Call me.

I called him.

"Daph," he said. "Are you OK? Where are you?"

I swallowed. "I'm at the hospital," I said. I could feel the tears building. I squeezed my eyes shut. I wanted to tell him the truth. I wanted to so badly. But I was too scared. Too afraid this might be our last call, and then? "My dad is having some tests run."

"Jesus, Daph. Cedars? I'm getting in my car."

"No," I said. "You can't. He doesn't want anyone here."

I could feel the hot sting of a riptide. I kept them shuttered.

"I'm not coming for him," Hugo said. "I'm coming for you."

I moved my arm, and a needle pulled at my vein. I wanted to unstring myself from this hospital bed and run. Run as fast and as far as I could before, what? My heart gave out? At least I'd be in motion.

And then I thought about what it would be like to be in Hugo's arms right now. To have him crawl into this hospital bed and hold me. To press my face into the warmth of his chest and forget who I was, what body I possessed, that my number might be called. I could feel it physically—my desire for him to be there. I wanted to tell him to come.

Hurry. I need you.

But I couldn't. Hugo did not know. I had never told him this giant piece of my puzzle. And introducing him to this—to all the complications of it, now—did not seem possible. Our time was almost up.

"I'll call you later," I said. "Please, don't come here. We're OK."

"Daphne."

A long silence. I couldn't talk, I knew I'd cry.

"You'll keep me posted?"

My voice caught in my throat. I forced it out, unwavering. "Of course."

During my first hospital stint, when we found out something was wrong, my parents met with the doctors alone. They'd have pre-meetings, where they'd discuss the course of action and then present it to me, united. I still remember my mother's tight smile.

But I also remember the day after I was admitted. I had gotten up to use the restroom, and my door was cracked open. My father was gone, but my mother was in the hallway, so was Dr. Frank. We didn't know him yet, he was just a crotchety man with a goatee.

"But what about advancements in medication?" my mother was asking. "Trials. You should see how good her immune system is. She never gets sick. Not even a cold!"

"Every year there's more and more. And that will definitely play a role."

"If there's something broken, can't we fix it? She could do surgery, we'd get her the very best physical therapy. I don't understand, you see. She's healthy . . ."

I heard the desperation in her voice, the pleading. I understood that she was walking her palms along the walls, trying to find the latch to the door. Surely there had been some mistake. Surely not her daughter. She wanted an exit, an answer. She wanted this to go away immediately and have everything whole again. Healthy.

I heard Dr. Frank leave and then my mother's ragged breathing by the door. The short, hollow sobs. They felt like a knife in my stomach. I was doing this to her. I was causing her this pain, this grief. It was impossible. It wasn't right. When she came back inside, her face was smiling, but her hands were shaking. I'd never forget their movement, like hummingbirds.

There is nothing more terrifying than lying in a hospital bed and knowing your mom can't fix it. That she can't make it better. That no amount of bargaining with any doctor will carry you—the both of you—to safety.

I could hear Hugo's breathing on the other end—hovering, waiting. I hung up the phone.

The next day I went into surgery. My mom pressed her lips to my forehead. She smelled like lavender and cabbage, like always.

"We'll see you soon," she said. Her eyes were glassy, but her face was steady. She was practiced.

"We love you," my father said.

"I want a cookie tonight," I said.

My father squeezed my hand. "You got it."

They inserted the stent, traveled it up through my groin and the veins of my body into my heart, and then opened it—pop—at precisely the right angle. It went off without a hitch. I woke up groggy but otherwise untouched. I could read it on my mother's face that everything had gone well; I didn't even need to hear her words.

"You did it," she said, her face on mine. "Great work, baby girl. Everything is OK."

They kept me overnight for monitoring, and I went home the next day, ahead of schedule.

I was released, as I had been many times before, into the care of my parents. Into the spare bedroom in their house in the Palisades. One that should have been a gym or an office but they kept with a queen bed, because they had to. Into homemade low-sodium chicken noodle soup and *The Devil Wears Prada* and my dad's peanut butter chocolate chunk cookies. My parents resumed their roles as medication administrators and temperature takers and phone command—messaging our team of doctors any unusual updates. They were pros, my parents. They had PhDs in caregiving now.

I had told Hugo that my father was out of the hospital—it was not *technically* a lie. And that I was going to be at their house for the next two or three days. He called, but I did not pick up. I didn't want to talk to him until I knew what to say, until I hoped I wouldn't have to lie any more than I already had. Until I could truly figure out just how I was going to continue to keep this from him.

I felt better quickly. I was used to surgery, was used to my body being strung up, marionetted, foreign parts and substances swimming in my veins. I didn't know if my will was strong or if my baseline had been torpedoed or if it was just being young, but I bounced back fast. By the next day I was up and moving around, pouring my own orange juice and commanding the remote.

My dad was on his morning run—his first of the week. He'd been standing vigil in the living room, at the ready for anything

I might need. And my mom was in the garden. I could tell they were trying to give me space, while still being around.

The house was empty when he showed up at the door. I heard the knocking and thought it must be Joan, over to deliver another round of muffins.

"Hugo."

"Hi," he said. He stood there in jeans and a white polo T-shirt. His hair had no product in it, and it hung in tufts.

"What are you doing here?"

"You haven't answered any of my calls," he said. "I've been extremely worried about you all."

I noticed then that he was carrying a gigantic bouquet of flowers—white roses and purple lilacs and tendrils of green ferns.

I had on sweatpants and a sweatshirt. It was January in Los Angeles—sunny and cold.

"We're totally fine. You didn't need to come here."

"You won't answer me." He leaned in closer. He looked like he hadn't slept. "I want to be there for you."

Hugo offered the flowers to me, but I could not take them, they were too heavy—a thick ceramic vase held them together. They looked like they weighed thirty pounds.

"They're beautiful," I said. I shook my head.

"Daph," Hugo said. "How is he?"

And that's when my dad came jogging up the steps, fresh off his run, his baseball cap lined with sweat.

"Hey," he said. "Hugo! What a nice surprise."

Hugo looked from me to my dad and back again. I could see the confusion in his eyes, trying to compute what he was seeing.

"Do you want to come in?" My dad jogged up a few more steps and put a hand on Hugo's shoulder.

Hugo shook his head. "It's nice to see you, Mr. Bell. You must be feeling better."

My dad cocked his head at Hugo and then turned his attention to me. He nodded once, slowly. He understood. This was not the first time.

"All right," my father said. "I'm going to head inside. Would you like me to take these?" He did not wait for a response but plucked the flowers out of Hugo's arms and disappeared through the door.

When he was gone, Hugo turned to me. He didn't say anything, just looked at me. I could see it all there—his confusion and bewilderment and the pain of being lied to.

I felt a rage seize up in me. The unjustness of it all. The anger at my father being able to run, to jog up these stairs so freely and easily. The fire at Hugo just showing up, thinking it was simple. That whatever flimsy emotion he was feeling mattered, *could* matter. That all he had to do was get me through this little rough patch and we could go back to brunch.

Everyone had a body that worked. Everyone but me.

"Do you want to tell me what's going on?" Hugo asked. He didn't sound angry, not exactly. He sounded measured. If I'm honest, he sounded scared. He knew now that I had been lying, he knew whatever it was wasn't small.

I didn't want to tell him. I didn't want to tell anyone. I had made it to twenty-eight without ever revealing my diagnosis to a single person I dated. I hid my illness in quiet corners, wrote my scars off as ancient relics, rolled my eyes at exercise. But I couldn't now. I'd been caught. And I didn't know how to get out of it—the answer was, I wasn't strong enough to climb.

"Yes," I said. "I just need a few minutes. Can you meet me at my apartment tonight?"

"No," Hugo said. He wasn't angry or harsh or even impatient. "I want to know what's going on now."

I sat down on the stone steps. All at once, it felt too hard to stand. Like gravity was pulling me down, pulling me toward the center—folded in two, where I belonged. "I'm sick," I said.

Hugo's gaze softened, but he didn't say anything, not right away, then: "And I'm guessing it's not the flu."

I laughed. I didn't mean to. It came out in a short burst of air. "No," I said. "Not that. I have a heart condition."

I had told so few people the truth in my life, but I had said those words so frequently. To new doctors, to nurses drawing blood, to teachers, administrators, once, to the postman about a particularly heavy Amazon box. But I had never told someone I might love.

"Daphne," he said. "Like from when you were young? What kind of heart condition?"

"I had a sudden cardiac arrest when I was twenty. The kind that most people don't survive."

"Jesus."

"I was in and out of the hospital for two years after. I have a congenital heart disease, which means it was there since birth, I just didn't know it. My heart doesn't work very well."

He pointed to my chest. "Your scar," he said.

I nodded.

"I just had a stent put in my heart," I said. "That's why I was at the hospital. I have no idea what the future holds, Hugo, but for the past eight years, it hasn't looked very good."

Hugo looked at me. Not in horror, exactly, but in bewilderment. Like I was a stranger. Like he was trying to remember my full name. I felt my hands go numb and cold.

"Why didn't you tell me?"

I shook my head. "I had no idea how to say what I just did to you."

Hugo nodded. "I'm sorry," he said. "Shit. Daphne." He shifted his body weight from one foot to the other. He looked at me, then up at my door.

I felt him wanting to run, and that suggestion of movement, that longing to disengage, broke my fucking heart.

"I don't know what to say."

The almighty Hugo was speechless, because he couldn't deal with this. Of course he couldn't. It's too big for anyone; that's why I tell no one.

Three months.

I felt the fluttering in my chest, the emotion rising from my shitty, fucked-up heart to my throat.

"I think this has to end," I told him.

Hugo snapped his gaze to mine. "No way," he said. "Did I say that? That is not what I want. I'm just trying to wrap my head around—"

"It's fine," I said. "You should go."

"Daphne, stop. Let's talk about this. You just came at me with a lot of information. I want to talk about it. I want to understand."

"Hugo," I said, "there's nothing to talk about."

He fought me on it. He said he just needed some time, that

he wanted to figure out how to be there for me, with me. But as much as I was afraid of losing him, the thought of him being with me out of pity was impossible. I couldn't bear that I'd have him and always know, somewhere, that he had signed up for someone healthy, and what he got was me.

"Why are you doing this?" Hugo asked me. "We're just getting started."

"Because our time is up," I said. I made a move to stand, Hugo came closer to me.

"Bullshit," he said. "Says who?"

I do not know what prompted what happened next. I do not know if I was delirious or devastated or just hopped up on medication, but I told him. The thing I had never shared with a single other person on earth. Not my parents, not Kendra, not Irina, not the postman. I told him about the papers.

"I get pieces of paper that tell me exactly how long I'll spend with a man, and our paper said three months. We've been together for three months today."

He was quiet for a long time. I thought he was going to tell me I was crazy, or worse, try to humor me. *Can I see them? Whose handwriting?* But instead, for the first time since he'd gotten there, he sat down on the stone step next to me. He ran a hand over his forehead and kept it there.

"Christ," he said.

I felt something tighten in my chest, down deep into the muscle. The heart doesn't often hurt. The illness comes out in other ways. In the blue tint of hands and lips, in the shortness of breath, in the swelling of my legs, in the brain fog, too. And close, in the chest. But the heart itself rarely hurts. You rarely feel it at all.

"I wish I would have known," he said.

"What?"

"That it was finite for you."

I swallowed. I wanted to cry, but I thought if I did I might never stop.

"No," I said. "Trust me. It's better to not know it's coming."

Hugo smiled at me, but it was sad, worn. "Spoken like someone who has never experienced the alternative."

Chapter Twenty-Seven

I tell Jake I'll move in with him the following week. My lease is up at the end of the month, and suddenly life is comprised of comparing moving company quotes and going through my closet, deciding how many hooded sweatshirts and cross-body bags one woman can own.

"I cleared out half the closet for you," Jake says when I'm over that Saturday night. He's pouring me a glass of sparkling water, and we're waiting for a Mozza pizza delivery. I'm snacking on some of Mrs. Madden's most recent batch of cookies, curled up on the couch.

"I'm probably going to need two-thirds," I say. "I'm putting a lot in storage, but I have an alarming number of shoes."

Jake laughs.

"I like your shoes. Come here. I want to show you something."

He holds out a hand to me and pulls me up off the couch.

"I was comfortable," I say, already unfurling myself.

"It'll be worth it, I promise."

Jake leads me into the second bedroom. When I see what he's done, I'm speechless. Usually there's a couch and some exercise gear in there—and a television on a console against the main wall. All of that is gone. Instead, there are built-in shelving units, a beautiful mahogany desk, and a CB2 gold-and-oatmeal office chair. A maroon velvet love seat replaces the oversize couch.

"I wanted you to have somewhere that was just your own," he says. "I know you value your space, so I wanted you to have it here, too. Just because we're living together doesn't mean you have to stop being who you are."

I don't know what to say. He's transformed this space for me. I am overwhelmed by this gesture, the incredible man before me.

"Jake," I say. "This is amazing."

Jake takes my hand and leads me to the love seat. He strokes my fingers.

"I want you to know that this is serious for me. Not in a scary way, just—I really want to be with you. And to make all the commitments you can make to another person."

I peer at him. "Are you proposing to me?"

He's silent for a moment. "No," he says. "But I hope I will, someday."

I swallow. It's everything I want to hear, of course. It's everything any girl would want to hear. He's generous and kind, and he's transformed his antiseptic man cave into a room of my very own.

"If there's something holding you back, you can tell me," he says. "In fact, now would be the time."

"What do you mean?"

Jake looks at me. He runs a hand from my shoulder down

to my wrist and then holds my hand there. "Sometimes I feel like you have this other life I know nothing about. When you're not here you're just—I can feel it, you're floating above us. And I want to be let in, into your whole life. All of it. I realize this is very bad movie dialogue. I see that. Wow, yeah, you can feel when it's cringy— What I'm trying to say is, I want your honesty. I can handle your honesty."

I take a breath. And then I prepare to tell him the thing I have avoided for so long. The thing I have only ever told one other man, a very long time ago.

"I love you," I say. I look into his eyes and see the spark there, the relief and joy those words illicit in him. I say it again. "I love you, Jake."

He smiles. He takes my face in his hands. "I really like hearing that," he says. "You have no idea how much."

Chapter Twenty-Eight

"I have to tell him."

Hugo and I are seated at Verve Coffee on Melrose, Murph's leash tied to my chair. It's a fancy coffee house that in New York would be a postage stamp and here takes up half a block. We're at a table outside, on the deck. I have a specialty iced tea—some flavor called Huckleberry—and Hugo's sipping from an iced espresso.

"Yeah," he says. "You should, shouldn't you?"

I nod.

Hugo and I forwent our Sunday farmers market and instead got coffee. It's late for him, well past ten in the morning. It has been months since we've been alone together, and it feels good to be in his presence. I still get the same feeling of confidence from him I always do, and right now, I need it.

"What's holding you back?" Hugo asks. "You already told the guy you're moving in with him. Didn't he build you a bedroom?"

"It's an office."

"Whatever."

I sip from my iced tea. I'm wearing a white T-shirt, denim shorts, and sandals and I'm still hot. It's eighty degrees in the middle of March. The sun is shining. Everywhere people are emerging in bare legs and broad smiles as if summer is upon us.

Hugo has on a gray T-shirt and shorts. A baseball cap hides his forehead. He taps a foot under the table.

"What's holding me back?" I ask.

I look at Hugo and raise my eyebrows. It takes him a moment to get it, and when he does, he shakes his head. "Come on," he says. "That's not fair."

"It's the only history I have with this particular revelation."

"Yeah, OK. But was I an asshole about it? That's not how I remember it."

"We broke up."

"Daphne, please. You broke up with me." Hugo sets down his drink. "I'll give you that I was caught off guard. You kept secrets from me, and it threw me for a loop. I felt like I didn't know you; it fucked me up momentarily."

"You weren't scared by the fact that I kept secrets. You were scared by the secret."

Hugo looks at me point-blank. "I was scared by it all. Your heart, your ability to hide shit from me, the fact that you clearly didn't trust me." He sighs. "But if you want someone who isn't going to be afraid, you already have him. We're talking about this like we don't already know how he's going to react. It's obvious, Daph."

I press the icy cup between my palms. "What is?"

"Jake is the guy who is not going to be afraid. He's not going to fuck it up. He's not going to say the wrong thing, or run, or be an asshole. He loves you. He's going to look you straight in the eye and say he's all in."

I swipe a bead of condensation onto my pinky finger. "How can you be so sure? This is a huge deal. He lost his wife—"

"I've seen how he looks at you," Hugo cuts me off. "And it's just who he is. You know that, and I know that. The man is built for being a safety net."

"He's not a safety net," I say.

"It's not negative, Daph. I'm just saying he's going to show up for you."

I think about Jake on the love seat, asking me to confess myself, my literal heart.

"I think you're right."

"I know I am."

Hugo downs the rest of his drink. He sets it on the table with some force. "So just tell him and live happily ever after."

"That simple?"

He shrugs. "Why not?"

I run my teeth over my bottom lip. "Maybe ever after is only a few years. Maybe it's just a few months."

Hugo crosses his arms. When he looks at me, his gaze is dead center. "You have to stop believing the worst in everyone. Fuck, Daphne. You have to stop believing the worst in yourself."

I feel my throat constrict, the stinging behind my eyes. "Am I a terrible person? Seriously, Hugo, am I going to hell for this?"

I know what I expect him to say. I expect him to tell me that of course I'm going to hell, but who cares, because he'll be right there with me. But instead Hugo shakes his head and then closes his eyes into a smile.

When he opens them, he leans forward, toward me. The stools are low, and the round table is small. I can feel his knee knock into my shin.

"No," he says. His voice is calm, steady. "You're not a terrible person. You deserve to be happy, Daphne. Just let yourself be happy."

He keeps looking at me with this sincerity that I've never seen before from him.

"Is that what you want?" I ask. The words just tumble out, before I can stop them. They surprise me. They don't seem to surprise Hugo.

He exhales. "Honestly, Daph," he says. "This isn't about me. If you're looking for an excuse to run, you won't find it here. I'm not going to give you that."

I blink at him. "When did you become so mature?" I ask.

He sits back. He picks up his coffee. "I guess a lot really can happen in five years."

Chapter Twenty-Nine

Jake takes it exactly as Hugo said he would. He is kind and understanding and supportive. He makes me tea and strokes my hand and tells me that he isn't afraid. Of course he's not. He's Jake.

"I just don't understand why you didn't tell me sooner," he says.

"I've never told anyone," I tell him.

He pauses for a moment. "Not even Hugo?"

"He found out when I got sick again."

He disregards that news quickly. It's not about that. "I'm very sorry you've been dealt this," he says. "But I also want you to know that I love all of who you are."

"It's OK if you have questions."

"I do, and also, they're not changing anything."

He wants to know details. He wants to know about my full history and the schedule of testing. He wants to come to the appointments now. *We are in this together.*

"You're not alone," he tells me. He says it more than once.

I pack up the Gardner Street apartment—all the messy details of nearly a decade of life. Old vases and plates and piles of records. All of it comes with me, most of it to a storage unit in Hollywood and some to my parents' house.

"Are you sure you don't want the bookcase?" my mother asks me.

Jake carries it in and sets it down in their living room.

"No room, Mom."

"It is a nice one, but, yes, sadly we're at capacity." Jake takes the corner of his shirt up and wipes his face.

"I'm getting water!" my mother says.

She runs out of the room, and I follow her. Jake goes to the car for another box.

"It's a lot of stuff," she says, watching him out the window. "You won't miss it?"

"I shouldn't even have it," I say. "I didn't have room for it to begin with."

She tucks an arm around my waist. "I love your things. They are who you are."

I watch Jake grab an old lamp with a hula dancer for a base. My mom sees, too.

"Well, maybe not all of them."

She pours me a glass of water and then fills one for Jake. "Here, take it to him."

"Thanks, Mama."

She smiles. "You haven't called me that in a long time."

"I know."

She takes my face in her hands. Her fingers are cold from the water. "I like what I see," she says.

"Me?"

"You're doing good. Happy. And if you're happy, that's everything in the world to me."

"He's a good guy," I say.

My mother motions me out of the kitchen; Jake is back at the door, struggling with a nightstand.

"You're not so bad yourself," she says.

I move into Wilshire Corridor the last week of March. Mrs. Madden drops off cookies and brisket to celebrate my arrival.

"Your own Brisket Brigade," Jake tells me. "And you didn't even have to die first."

He looks at me, wide-eyed, and then we both start laughing—rolling, belly-hearty sobs. Jake grabs on to the wall to steady himself.

It's easy to tell Kendra then, too. Or, it's easier. My voice still shakes, and I still don't make direct eye contact, but it's not as hard as I thought it would be. People want to be there.

I unpack my mismatched dishware into Jake's kitchen, and my oversize towels into the bathroom. Murphy claims the spot by the window that gets the most sun.

Jake watches me set my trinkets—an ashtray from a trip to Portland, a Chinese famille rose porcelain box I bought on 1stDibs—on the coffee table, the mantel, any surface I can cover.

"You weren't kidding," Jake notes, handing me a glass of water. "You have a lot of stuff."

"Online shopping is easy to do from anywhere."

Jake nods. "Well, in that case," he says, "bring on the tchotchke!"

Three weeks after we get settled into what is now our apartment—after I cram what I can into the office den and fill the living room with way too many lamps, Jake and I leave the dogs at home and drive out to Malibu to have dinner at Moonshadows on the water. We're well into spring now, and the sun is setting later and later. As we drive out to the beach, the ocean on the left-hand side, I'm met with a revealing gratitude for this place, this city I call home.

When we arrive for dinner at 6:00 p.m., the sun is still high in the sky. Moonshadows hangs over the water—a glass-encased restaurant with a deck along the ocean. We get a table outside, right at the edge, so close that when the waves come in, we can feel the sea spray. I slip an old cashmere cardigan around my shoulders.

We order oysters and champagne and watch as the sky fades from brilliant blue to hazy shades of pink and lavender and tangerine. The beauty of the water, the proximity to this much nature, is so peaceful.

"Hey," Jake says. "I wanted to ask you something."

I know as soon as he says it. I have known for weeks, now. From when he told me he wanted to go to dinner in Malibu—the advance of the plan, the odd formality of deciding what and where we were eating, the fact that he confirmed I was still up for it on three separate occasions. But as I see him sitting across from me I realize it doesn't matter. It doesn't matter that I knew, that I anticipated this, that I saw it coming. Nothing, exactly, can prepare you for when these moments arrive.

"Yes?"

Jake is wearing a white button-down and light jeans. He has on loafers, a gift from my father. His freckles are fully in bloom. He looks charming and handsome—his long ears and curved nose and bright blue eyes. All the little details of significance, of someone significant.

He takes my hand from across the table. My stomach clenches, thinking he might get down on one knee, but he doesn't. He just holds my fingers in his palms—delicately and carefully.

"I love you," he says. "And I told you before I'm not really in the business of casual. I hope I've proven to you that I want to be here, and that I am."

I think about Jake getting me water every night before bed. I think about him putting my towel in the dryer if he knows I'm going to take a morning shower. Driving to my monthly bloodwork, now. All these small ways he shows he cares.

"Yes," I say.

He smiles at me. The smile of assurance, warmth. It's a smile of certainty. "Daphne," he says, "will you marry me?"

There is only one answer to this question.

"Yes."

Jake's face flushes with relief and pride and the purest joy, so exquisite I want to bottle that, this look on his face.

All my life I believed that it was the person who mattered, that once you met "the one" you'd enter through a magical door where it was all on the table. I see him holding it, now. I see everything he has to offer inside. I see a life.

He puts a small box on the table. I peel open the top. Inside is an emerald with a pave diamond band. It's modern, beautiful, and a little bit badass. It's perfect for me, honestly. Now that it's here, I can't imagine anything else.

"I love it," I say.

Jake smiles. "Kendra helped me pick it out."

He plucks the ring out of the box. I hold out my hand.

"Here."

It fits exactly right. I lift it up to the deepening sky, right over the horizon. The emerald catches the last brilliant rays of the disappearing sun.

Chapter Thirty

I show up to work the next day to find that Irina has erected a CONGRATULATIONS, GRADUATE! banner over the kitchen island. There are balloons and a giant Ring Pop, the size of my hand.

"Wow," I say. "Word travels fast."

"Kendra called," she says. "Let me see it."

I hold my hand out to her, and she surveys it, flipping my wrist back and forth like she's a doctor at an exam.

"So fine; it's gorgeous. He's like perfect or something?"

"Or something," I say.

Irina hands me a coffee that has just finished in the Nespresso. I set my bag on a stool and lean over the counter.

"And he took it like a champ," she says. It's not a question. It's a reminder, maybe.

I look at her. She's got on high-waisted jeans and a white bodysuit. Her hair is pulled back in a low bun. She doesn't have a stitch of makeup on, and her skin is flawless—radiant and rosy.

"You know, until Jake you were the only one besides my family, Hugo, and some friends from college who knew about my heart."

Irina nods. "It's my trustworthy face," she deadpans. "And the fact that I made you fill out insurance forms."

I shake my head. "No. You never treated me any differently. You never made me feel like I had something to make up for, or that there were things I couldn't do."

"You can't pick out a proper handbag," Irina says, gesturing to the leather satchel that's with me. "So I'd hold on to some modesty."

I shake my head. "That's not what I mean."

Irina touches my hand. "I know what you mean," she says. "But this relationship is like fight club. It works because we don't talk about it."

She turns around, back to the sink, and sets her coffee cup inside.

"I love you," I tell her.

"Oh, Daphne," she says, her back still to me. "Don't be obvious."

And then she turns around. I see a smile creep onto her face.

"You are one of the people I love most in this world. It should be self-evident. But—" She holds my gaze; I see just the slightest film on her eyes. "There you go."

It feels good to say it. It feels good to hear it. All this easy intimacy I denied myself for so long.

When I first met Kendra, I hadn't gotten close with a single person outside Tae and my family for years. I was in a glass bubble. I had friends, but they didn't understand my reality, and as the years wore on, we kept in touch less and less. I sidelined their friendship because I knew, somewhere deep down, that my life would never resemble theirs. That I may never get married; that I wouldn't carry children; that I'd only progress to the middle. I didn't want the comparison shoved in my face every day. I didn't want to look at them and feel ugly or resentful. I didn't want to see that the people I'd started with were already somewhere I'd never be.

And then there was Kendra. Maybe it was that she was alternative, that her life with Joel was narrated with happenstance instead of intention, or that she never questioned my life, just kept showing up, but our friendship was easy to maintain. She cracked the window. Irina flew in and blew down the door.

"What's going on with Penelope?" I ask Irina now.

Irina rolls her neck out. "What is always going on with Penelope," she says. "A lot of love and not as much compatibility. You think when you get to a certain age you figure it out, but life is much more like a continuum than a three-act structure. Here's the thing no one tells you in any of these fucking movies we make: love is not enough."

"No one wants to hear that," I say. "It's not sexy."

"You need so much more than love," she says. "Are you kidding? I'd love to be with someone who didn't sleep until ten a.m. Or who understood the importance of a clean house. Or who didn't splash water all over the bathroom sink when she brushed her teeth."

I laugh. "You think you'll ever go searching for someone who doesn't?"

Irina kneads a muscle in her neck. "The problem with love is that it's not enough," she says. And then she looks up at me. Her eyes are still soft. "But it's also nearly impossible to let go of once you've found it."

I straighten up.

"Well, that is a catch-22," I say.

Irina nods. She plucks a crumbled dish towel off the counter and begins to fold it. "Life is a catch-22," Irina says. "That's why God invented female friendship."

Chapter Thirty-One

Josh, six months.

After my breakup with Tae I stayed in Los Angeles for another year. There was an easing out of constant hospital living. I still had to do all the appointments and tests and blood draws, but we were no longer in constant-crisis mode and instead in a sort of homeostasis. There was a hovering, some space, and I wanted to fill it.

On the eve of my twenty-fourth birthday, I moved to San Francisco. I had gotten the job at Flext, a tech-venture start-up that was looking to revolutionize how people worked out at home. It was pre-Peloton, and they were getting a lot of buzz.

I'd first heard about the start-up from Alisa, my old college roommate. It was a friend of hers from New York's venture, and she asked me if I wanted to be an assistant there. They were looking for someone with a communications background who didn't mind the grunt work and the long hours. It sounded perfect.

"The only catch is, it's in San Francisco," Alisa said.

"Even better."

All during my years of dating Tae when he was at Stanford, I'd hear about the glory of San Francisco. It felt like a city comprised of everything off-limits. Hilly neighborhoods, bike rides, drinks at the top of skyscrapers, meetings on scooters.

We talked about my visiting often, but something always got in the way. I couldn't fly; it wasn't safe. There was another appointment. *What if something happened?*

Something always did.

But now I was free. I could visit if I wanted to. Hell, I could live there. So I did just that, I moved.

I met Noah the second night I was there, in that tiki bar down the block from the hotel where I was staying, and our five weeks together sped by with all the particularity of a film dissolve. When it ended, I was sadder than I should have been. And then I met Josh.

Josh was my boss. He was twenty-nine, with a 4.0 from Harvard and a hundred million dollars in venture capital. He was on fire. *Forbes* had just written a piece about him. He was being followed by *The New Yorker* for a three-month interview. He was poised to become Silicon Valley's next billionaire. To me, he just seemed like a guy in a J.Crew ad.

I walked into Flext's offices that day in jeans, a collared shirt, and so much enthusiasm I felt like a different person. I was excited to be there. The offices were an open-floor plan—no one had a door. Josh sat in the middle of the bullpen, typing away at his computer.

"That's our founder," Janelle, the receptionist, told me. "He's hot, right?"

Josh had auburn hair and green eyes, and everything about him felt congruent, all his features working together to present a unified image. He was like a completed puzzle. Symmetrical. Organized.

"Josh," Janelle said. "This is Daphne, our new assistant from Los Angeles."

Josh blinked once, as if pulling out of a trance, and then looked at me. "Hi," he said. "Daphne from Los Angeles."

I nodded.

"Glad to have you on board. I'm told you're good with Excel, that will come in handy. We're a tech start-up that isn't very high-tech."

I laughed. "Happy to help."

I didn't report to Josh. Instead, I reported to Tanaz, a twenty-eight-year-old who could code better than anyone I'd ever met. In college my sophomore-year roommate had been a computer science major. I had absorbed a few things by osmosis during our year together, and I could tell Tanaz was better than anyone.

It soon became clear to me that my job was mostly to make sure Tanaz never needed anything so she could continue to do what she did so well.

I began to anticipate her rhythms—when she'd want coffee, lunch, even a bathroom break. And I liked her, too. She started calling me "DB."

"It's shorter," she said. "And I like it more."

She made me call her "Tanz."

One syllable saves time.

I loved it there because it was a place where no one knew. I felt like a superhero, but instead of hiding a power I was hiding my illness. For the first time in nearly three years no one saw me as being sick. I was just a part of something. Normal. It felt incredible.

Josh and I didn't really speak until I'd been at Flext almost six weeks. At that point I was living in the Financial District simply because I'd found a cheap sublet. It was about an hour from the office but an easy drive. I'd taken my car with me up to San Francisco because I knew I'd never be able to walk the hills, and nothing made me happier than the freedom being behind the wheel afforded. I was in control, finally, again.

Flext's offices were in Palo Alto, and if I ever didn't feel like driving (which I rarely did) there was a direct train that the company reimbursed me for.

I hadn't been with Noah often during our five-week stint, and once it ended, I'd stay at the office late. I had gotten the paper a week earlier. It was sitting in the printer when I went to scan something: *Josh, six months.*

I was elated. Not necessarily about Josh, but about the length.

Six months felt like forever. I could swim in that much time. I could bathe in it.

Whatever stragglers were around in Flext's office after hours started having dinner together. There were only twenty-five employees in the office, and everyone knew one another, especially because there were no office doors. We'd order in—salads, tacos, pizza—and eat in a huddle—Parmesan packs and napkins littering the railing.

One particular Thursday evening Josh joined us. He sat with Tanaz, and then when he stood to get a napkin, we made eye contact. I waved.

"How's it going?" he asked. "Sorry things have been so hectic around here. I hope you're enjoying at least some of it?"

I swallowed my pizza. "No, it's good," I said. "Great, actually."

It was true. I was happy. I loved the schedule, the rhythm, and I loved how people relied on me. After so many years of feeling like a victim—always having to accept help—it felt good to be able to provide some.

There was an HR department, comprised of one person, Kelly, and she knew about my condition. If I had to come in an hour late or leave for a blood draw, it was always kosher.

"I like to get to know everyone who comes in, but things have been so crazy lately," Josh said. He looked at me. "I'm sorry."

"Don't be," I said. "I get it."

"Want to grab a bite?" Josh swung his arm out, inviting me into his section of the bullpen. I grabbed my pizza box.

He was relaxed—that was the thing that struck me first about him, how casual he was. In an industry and business that is neurotic and wired nearly all the time, he was like a raft on a lake. I could barely see him move.

"I know you're from LA," he said. "And that's where my knowledge evades me."

"Born and raised in the Palisades."

Josh folded a slice in half. I watched the grease funnel down into his napkin. "We lived in Sherman Oaks when I was a little kid, but then my folks moved to Hawaii."

"Hawaii?"

He took a bite, chewed through it. "I know. Everyone always asks me what growing up there was like, but honestly it's not that different from everywhere else."

"I feel like that was true of Malibu, too. The Palisades was suburban but still close to the ocean. People would ask me if I surfed all the time."

"Did you?"

"Not well."

Josh smiled, wiped his mouth. "Do you miss it?"

"The ocean?"

Josh shrugged. "Home."

I took a small bite of pizza. "Not right now."

Josh laughed. "One thing that's nice about the start-up life is that it doesn't matter that San Francisco sucks, you never have time to hang out in it anyway."

"So is work what you do for fun?"

Jake smiled. "Indeed," he said. "I'm honestly not sure I could sketch my apartment from memory. I broke up with someone last year, and my life has been kind of all work since." He looked at me, alarmed. "Sorry if that's too much information."

"That you're single?" I asked. "I can handle it."

Flext's office was incredibly close-knit—everyone was friends. It felt halfway between pulling an all-nighter in college and summer camp. Both things I had, confessionally, enjoyed. I loved the energy of it. Whole hours would go by where I'd forget the past two years.

I was the one who asked Josh out first.

We were at a company happy hour, at a karaoke bar not too far from my apartment, as it turned out. It was called Karaoke One, and it had a neon sign that read: OPEN YOUR WALLET. YOUR MOUTH IS YOUR CHOICE.

We got a room in the back that was covered in geometric-print wallpaper. It would have made me feel claustrophobic if I hadn't kicked that fear somewhere around my eighth MRI scan—being forced into small, confined spaces regularly made me adapt.

Josh got up to sing a Pat Benatar song. I liked him, that much I knew. I liked his ease, and how down-to-earth he seemed. It had been two weeks since the paper, and my crush had fully bloomed. I felt it was reciprocated, but it was hard to tell. Josh was a good boss and a great role model. I knew he'd never make the first move.

"'*We are young*,'" Josh sang.

Tanaz cupped her hands around her mouth and hollered into my ear.

"He's cute, huh?" she said to me.

I was staring.

"Yes." I didn't see the point in denying it. People met at work sometimes, didn't they?

"He was so torn up about his ex last year he barely came around. He seems happier since you got here." She smiled at me. "When you have so few people in the office, one person can really change the dynamic. And I think you changed ours in a great way." It was the longest conversation we'd ever had.

"'*Searching our hearts for so long.*'"

Someone handed me a beer. I took a swig. The bar was loud, and our room was small and crowded and hot. Everyone was sweating. I loved it.

"'*Love is a battlefield.*'"

When Josh passed the mic off to Janelle, he came down to Tanaz and me.

"How much did that suck?" he asked.

"You were bad," Tanaz said. "But you looked happy about it."

"Do you want to get a drink sometime?" I asked him.

He tilted his beer toward me. "No time like the present."

"That's not what I mean," I said.

"I know," Josh said.

Tanaz was making herself scarce.

"But I'm your boss."

"Do you like me?" I asked. I'd never been that bold before. It felt like adrenaline to the vein.

"I do," Josh said.

"So let's have a drink."

Josh eyed me. I could tell he wanted to.

"OK," he said.

Before anything—before we went out for that drink, or held hands, or even had a conversation with the door shut—which admittedly would have been difficult, again, there were no doors—we told our one-woman HR department, Kelly.

"Is that really necessary?" I asked Josh.

"This is a small company. Everything has to be aboveboard."

We signed a bunch of papers that I didn't read and Josh read thoroughly. "There's a clause in here that says if we stop dating for any reason she doesn't have to leave the company, correct?"

"She cannot be fired for your relationship," Kelly said. "Is that what you're asking?"

"I just want to make sure she is looked after."

It's just a drink, I thought.

It wasn't just a drink. After the papers were signed we went to Alchemist Bar & Lounge, a dimly lit bar near Oracle Park. We drank rye whiskey and apple brandy out of mason jars, and then we went back to Josh's apartment. He had a loft overlooking the bay that was sparsely decorated in a step up from IKEA furniture.

"I haven't had time to make it something. My ex did some decorating, but when we broke up, she took most of the things with her."

"I like it," I said. "You could throw a huge party here."

Josh laughed. "I've had a few company get-togethers. Not much as of late." He went over to the stainless steel refrigerator. "I have red or white, and they're both in the fridge because I know nothing about wine."

"Can I have a glass of water?"

Josh struck a hand to his face in a gesture that felt overly dramatic. "I'm so sorry, of course, I should have offered as soon as we got in."

He took a mini Brita out of his fridge and poured me a large glass.

"Thanks."

I took a few big gulps. He watched me.

"You're very interesting," he said. "You don't seem to have a whole lot of fear. Me on the other hand, I'm basically living in a Hitchcock movie."

I wiped my lips. "That is not true."

Jake shook his head. "No, it is. I mean, I'm not trying to invalidate your experience or anything, but that's how it reads to me. You seem very direct." He paused. "I like it."

I set the water glass down. I came around the counter to meet him by the sink.

"Hi," he said.

"Hi."

I put my hands on his chest. He was the same height as me. I didn't have to reach.

"Can I kiss you now?" I asked.

He shook his head. I could see his dimples. "Are you sure this is what you want?"

"Yes. If it would help, I can sign more papers. Maybe page eighty will give you a sense of security."

He put his hand around my waist and then pressed his lips against mine. The kiss was tame, chaste almost. A finger wiggled through an envelope seam.

It was the first relationship I'd ever had that moved so quickly legally but so slowly physically. After that night, we were just together. Nothing at the office changed; for the most part things were so busy there that interpersonal drama wouldn't even have been possible if we'd wanted it—there just wasn't enough time. But after work we'd often leave together, stopping off for a drink or going back to his place to cook a Blue Apron meal.

My health was stable, the job was fun and demanding, and Josh was a good boyfriend. He even met my parents when they came up one weekend.

"He's smart," my father said. "A very nice young man."

I thought he was a real grown-up. It felt so good and right to be in a committed relationship. I'd missed it with Tae, whatever poor man's version we got, and I relished all the things I was getting back now. The dinners out; the walking down the street, holding hands; the movies on the weekends. I loved thinking about how other people saw us. What we looked like to them.

We were normal. And normal felt better than good. Normal felt like heaven.

The thing that always made me pause, though, is that I

couldn't tell how much he liked *me*. It was like once he cleared it with work there were no more options, we were just going to date. I wasn't sure how much he wanted a girlfriend versus how much he wanted me to be his.

Six months in I got my answer. Things had taken a turn the week before at work. The round of investing had fallen through. Flext was running dangerously low on cash, and there were talks of layoffs. What had once seemed like the golden ticket now felt like it was possibly expired. We were all on eggshells, and Josh was the worst. Stressed and apologetic. He knew it was his responsibility to keep all these people employed and wasn't sure he'd be able to do it.

We were at dinner on a Tuesday when he told me. He'd been strange all day, but I assumed it was work, the hovering possibility of having to shut all of this down.

"I need to tell you something," he said. "I'm going to be getting back together with Emily."

He didn't pause; he just said it. I blinked at him. I had heard her name frequently in our time together, his ex, but I had no idea they were even in contact.

"Nothing has happened—I haven't cheated on you. I promise. I hope you'll believe me, although I'd understand if you don't. And if I could stop myself from feeling this way, I would. I don't want to hurt you. But we ran into each other on the train last week, and we got to talking, and I realized how much I still love her." He looked away. He was measured, but he was upset. "She feels the same way."

I believed him. Based off how he'd handled our beginning, I knew he was telling the truth.

"I don't know what to say," I said. I couldn't tell if I was devastated or just shocked. They felt like the same thing.

He shook his head. He ran his hands through his hair. "I know. Me either. I like you so much. We have such a great time together, and you're fun and—"

I held my hand up. I didn't think I could hear more.

"I just," he said. "She's the one."

What I knew then was this: he had clearly been in love with her the whole time. I didn't know if it was betrayal, but I knew it didn't feel good. Suddenly this bubble I'd created for myself—one without heartache—burst. I wasn't the anonymous feel-good girl from LA. I was a girl with a history, and he was a man who couldn't let go of his.

"I'm happy for you, then," I said. I didn't mean it. But I wanted to be mature. I wanted to, somehow, right the ship again. To put myself back in the driver's seat, to not feel at the mercy of someone else. I wanted to be in control.

"Do you really mean that?" He looked relieved. I couldn't understand how he could possibly be that stupid, how I hadn't known, how I had let so much time pass and ended up here. "Because I don't want you to go anywhere. The office needs you. You're an important part of our team."

"Yeah," I said. "Sure."

We didn't finish our dinner. When I got up, he didn't fight me on it. He didn't say, "Come on, eat your burger" or "One more drink" or "Let's just stay a bit longer." He didn't want to; it was obvious. He wanted to go home to her. All that was standing in between this bar and their reconciliation was me.

Josh asked if he could order me a car. I shook my head.

"See you Monday," he said. He sounded almost cheerful. I imagined him then, calling Emily. Telling her it had gone surprisingly well. I imagined her telling him to come over, quickly. All the lust and longing they'd buried down deep coming to the surface now. The relief they'd feel at finally getting to be together again. Heady, urgent kisses.

I had known, of course I had. I saw the paper. But time had gone too quickly. Six months into five minutes. I hadn't been paying attention. And then, I hadn't been ready.

I wasn't used to not being chosen, and I hated it. I hated feeling like someone else had the answers. Here, now, Josh had known things I didn't. It had only ever been the other way around.

I quit the following week—contracts are only good for problems in vacuums—and the start-up went belly-up the following year. I knew because I kept tabs on Flext and Josh—checking Instagram, googling keywords. Everyone was shocked and disappointed: the company that had shown such promise was dead in the water.

But a month after the dissolution of Flext, there was a wedding announcement: Josh and Emily had gotten married. A small outdoor ceremony at the bride's parents' house in Marin County. Only immediate family and a few close personal friends. A violinist played "Over the Rainbow" and Emily wore yellow flowers in her hair, per the *New York Times*. They looked radiant. In the attached photo, he was kissing her open palm.

I thought about what it would feel like to be that cherished, to be that chosen, and for the first time in my life, I knew I wanted it. I wanted epic love, the kind that's reserved for the movies. I wanted someone to speak about me the way I knew Josh spoke about Emily. I wanted rooftop nights and mornings in bed and the feeling of belonging. I wanted yellow flowers in my hair. I wanted everyone to look at me and him and say, "Isn't it ideal?"

But acknowledging a desire means acknowledging the what-if of that want. I wanted it, and that meant I was terrified—of never having it. Of never getting there.

It's a cliché to say you are scared of getting hurt. But what if the papers weren't just doling my life out in increments of time but also protecting me? From the pain of being blindsided. From never again having to say *I didn't see it coming.*

After Josh I vowed to be better about trusting the papers. If they did not say forever, I wouldn't invest. I would stay cautious, aware.

I would believe them.

Chapter Thirty-Two

A month after our engagement Jake tells me he thinks we should have a September wedding. We are sitting outside Alfred's coffee shop in Melrose Place, an upscale enclave that houses designer boutiques and way too many green-juice storefronts. All around us people in expensive activewear walk their midsize dogs. I'm drinking an iced oat milk latte, and Jake has a chagaccino—their signature drink made with monk fruit and mushroom. It's actually excellent, but some primal force makes me refuse to order it. A little too Live Laugh Love.

"Jake," I say. "That's less than four months."

The sun is strong overhead, and we both have our sunglasses on. I'm wearing denim shorts, an oversize white T-shirt, and Birkenstocks. I wiggle my toes against the leather straps.

Jake shrugs. "Does that seem too soon?"

"What's the rush?"

Jake takes a long sip. And then he folds his hands on the table. "I want to have a conversation I think we've been avoiding."

I press my palms around the plastic cup. I can feel my stomach start to hollow. "Yes?"

He exhales. "I want to talk about kids. I think we should."

When I told Jake about my heart, he had questions. I tried to answer them as honestly as possible, but the baby thing is hard. It isn't off the table, but it's also not advisable. And that's just from a medical perspective. There are many ways to have a child, I just never believed I'd make that choice.

"OK."

Jake takes my hand. His is cold, but so is mine. "This is not a pressurized conversation. At all. And we don't have to decide anything today. We can have another twenty of these."

"Sounds fun."

Jake remains serious. "I want you to be comfortable, Daphne. And I want us to be honest." He pauses. "But the truth is I need to better understand where you're at."

"With being able to do it?"

"With wanting it."

A twentysomething girl and guy walk up to the counter to order. She leans into him, checking her phone. It looks so uncomplicated, so easeful. I envy it.

"I don't know," I say. "I kind of decided it wasn't possible, and then I put it in a box, and I've never taken it out to think about whether I actually want it or not." I look down at my cup. The ice is melting, creating a translucent layer of dirty water at the top. "I'm not sure the answer is yes."

I don't look at him, but I feel him react. Because here's the truth, the thing neither of us is willing to say: Jake should be a father.

He should wake up for midnight feedings and research strollers and coach Little League teams. He should paper thighs with Band-Aids and make spaghetti five nights in a row. He should change diapers and set up plastic swing sets and fill up an iPhone with videos. He's that man. It's almost as if it's already happened.

"And I know you do," I finish.

"Daph—"

"It's OK," I say, looking up at him. "You said we should be honest."

Jake nods. I see him swallow. When he speaks, his tone is measured. "I do want it," he says. "I've always pictured myself as a father. But life hasn't turned out the way I imagined it. Not really at all."

There is a sadness in his voice, a sort of melancholy I don't normally see in him, not even when he speaks about her.

"You shouldn't have to give up the things you want," I tell him.

Jake smiles. He squeezes my hand. "I want you," he says.

When I was young, back when my heart was an illusion of health, I figured I'd become a mother. There was no real want or desire attached to it, maybe I was too young for that anyway, it just seemed obvious. At some point—some far-off point in the future—I'd fall in love and get married and have a baby.

But life took a detour. And since we veered off course I haven't spent a lot of time thinking about what I would have wanted if we hadn't. Does it matter? There is only this life. This very one we are living. And in this one, children never made their way in.

I kept expecting them to—to wake up one day and think: *I need this. Now.* But it hasn't happened yet.

"I think you have to really ask yourself if you can give that up," I say. "It's not a small thing."

Jake pauses, thoughtful. "So the answer is no? Is that what you're saying?"

"I'm saying I don't know if I'll ever want to open that box."

I can see Jake struggling, processing this, and part of me is angry. Because we're already engaged. Because he's already committed to this. Did he do it because he assumed I'd change my mind? *We'll get married, of course she'll want a baby.*

"Daphne," he says. He grabs both my hands in his. He looks straight into my eyes. "If all I got was you, it would be more than enough for me. I just want to know what you want your life to be like. I want you to always make choices based on what you want, not what you think you can or can't have."

He leans across and kisses me. I feel his lips on mine—solid and centered. But I can't help but feel as we sit there, the day passing all around us, that he doesn't get it. What I want doesn't exist. Not here, not in this life. And the next best thing is not ignoring that reality. The next best thing is acceptance of what is. If I can't be healthy, I do not want to pretend I am. I want the ease that comes from acknowledging that I'm not. I want the truth.

I often wonder what our responsibility is to other people, how much we owe them. Whose job is it to look out for our own happiness. Us, or the people who love us? It's both, of course. We owe ourselves and each other. But in what order?

As I look at Jake sitting across from me I feel the desire to protect him palpably—I feel it down deep into my bones. And then I consider something else, something that is hard to look at but impossible, now, to ignore. I wonder if I've been seeing that desire—honoring it, recognizing it—and calling it love.

Protection and love are not the same thing. Love says, *I will try and I will fail.* Love says, *Despite.* Love says, *And yet and yet and yet.*

And then I think about Jake, about everything he has endured, about everything that happened in his life before he ever met me. I wonder if we are both trying to rescue me, and what happens when we realize we cannot.

Chapter Thirty-Three

It's a hundred degrees outside."

Hugo and I are at the Silver Lake Reservoir, walking the flat loop with Murphy. The dog has a spring in his step today, and the pace is brisk. After a few minutes, I tug him to slow down.

It's after seven, but the sun is barely descending. It's almost summer in Los Angeles. Everywhere there is growth—the water is clear, the weeds are green and blowing in the breeze, and the flowers are little pops of yellow all around us. Overhead, a bird calls and dives, skimming the surface.

Jake is out of town for a few days on a work trip to New York, and I have the apartment to myself. So far it's been a lot of reality TV and takeout for one in the air-conditioning. Saber has shown no interest in leaving the cool sixty-eight degrees, so today it's just Murphy and me.

"Don't be dramatic," Hugo says. "It's seventy-eight, tops."

He's not wrong, but even in a sundress and sneakers, I'm sweating. I can feel beads of moisture hanging at my hairline.

This is mine and Hugo's first solo outing since Jake and I got engaged, which was a month ago already. I told him on the phone. He seemed genuinely happy for me. We've texted some, but things have been more reserved between us. I thought when I saw him today our behavior would be reflective of our online exchanges—short, no details—but he's still Hugo.

Jake and I haven't started planning a wedding, but we agree it should be small. Twenty people on the beach, maybe drinks and dinner after in the sand. No fuss. Not a lot of money spent. Just intimate and beautiful. Good food, good music, good wine.

"Well it *feels* like it's a hundred degrees."

Hugo looks at me, suddenly alarmed. "Are you OK?" he asks.

I side-eye him. "What do you mean by that?"

Hugo redirects his gaze to Murphy. "It's just a question."

"I'm fine," I say. I grab his arm and shake it back and forth. I see him relax. "I've honestly been feeling pretty good lately."

Hugo nods. Murphy has stopped walking, his ears pricked, and Hugo bends down to scratch his head.

"Hey, buddy," he says. "Hey, monsieur. Murph and turf."

Murphy looks up, somewhat wearily.

"Jake took him to the beach last weekend," I say. "He threw a stick, and Murphy just stared at it. I could fully hear his judgment. Jake still thinks there's a dog in there."

Murphy nuzzles into Hugo as he continues to rub his head, chin, the fur under his ears.

"How dare anyone treat you like an animal?" Hugo says. "The indignity. Don't they know you are a prince among men?"

Murphy steps out of Hugo's grasp, requiring some space, and Hugo straightens.

He's wearing olive-colored shorts and a gray T-shirt. His sunglasses are looped over the collar of his shirt, revealing a few chest hairs.

"So you're really going to do this?" he says.

I roll back my shoulders. "What do you mean?"

"You're really going to get married."

It's not a question, and it doesn't feel like one. He looks straight at me when he says it. We are not alone at the reservoir, but for sunset, it's not particularly crowded. A few runners jog by; a father pushes a stroller. But in this moment it feels like we're the only two people here.

"Why?" I ask. But it's not a question, either, not really.

"I guess I'm wondering if you're happy."

I blink at his question. *What?* "That's ridiculous," I say. "You're the one who *told* me to be happy."

Hugo nods. "I know I did. Yeah, I told you to embrace it." He clears his throat. He squints into the sun. "Was I right?"

"That I should be happy? I don't know, Hugo, feels like a good bet."

I cross my arms. Hugo drops his gaze down to mine.

"I've been thinking about what you said, about the day we broke up," Hugo says. "You were right. I couldn't handle it."

Despite the summer heat, I feel a cold chill go up my spine. "It doesn't matter. Hugo, this is ancient history." I start to walk again, tugging Murphy on. "It was so many years ago."

"Yes," Hugo says. "It does. I couldn't handle it back then. What you told me scared the shit out of me."

I stop abruptly. "OK, fine. You didn't like that I was sick. It doesn't matter—we're not together. Why are we even talking about this? You said yourself you weren't giving me any excuses."

"You're right," Hugo says. "I'm not here to give you excuses. But the truth is something different."

"Oh yeah?" I say. "And what's that?"

"You think I stopped giving a shit because we stopped sleeping together." Hugo stares at me. "The truth is I had to teach myself how to handle it because I didn't want to lose you."

Murphy starts tugging on the leash. He spots a bunny—his kryptonite. The only thing that will cause Murphy to behave with any semblance of animation. I hold firm to his leash.

I feel a righteous anger begin to burn in me. It ignites, straight out of my core.

"Do you want some kind of trophy or something? Congratulations, you figured out how to be friends with someone with a heart condition! I'll throw you a parade. How brave of you to confess that." I can also feel the venom rising in me. It feels vicious, poisonous. I want to eject it all.

Hugo looks agitated. "Fuck, Daph, will you just listen to me?"

"What?" I say. I can hear myself snarl. "Why are you doing this? What do you want? We're taking a *walk*, Hugo."

And then he stops. It's as if the whole world hovers. I can feel the stillness around us—the crest of a wave right before it curls and tumbles.

"You want to know what I want?" he says. He moves closer to me—so close I can feel his body—all of the tiny atoms vibrating to make Hugo, Hugo. "I want to take you home right now. I want to not let you sleep a single fucking wink tonight. I want to hold you and touch you and make up for five years of not doing either. And then I want to wake up with you and take you to breakfast, and I want to talk about where we should live and how we're going to fit all your shit there— Yeah, Daph, I want that. I want you. For as long as it lasts. Fifty years or five or fifteen fucking minutes."

My feet are rooted to the ground. My hands have gone entirely numb. From somewhere in the distance, I hear the call of a bird overhead.

"But you know what I want more than anything?" Hugo continues. "More than I even want you?"

The world seems to turn on its axis—I feel like we're all falling, hurtling toward an unexplored edge. I do not know how I could possibly answer. I do not know how I'll ever be able to speak again.

"I want the truth. I want the truth for you. For you, and for Jake, and for me, honestly. However inconvenient that shit is."

"You want the truth?" I say. I can feel the fire in me—building in my abdomen, making its way up my throat and out my mouth, now. Everything he feels so free to say. Everything I have to hold. "The truth isn't just inconvenient, Hugo. Do you know what the truth is? It's a death sentence when you're twenty years old. It's never being able to run a mile. It's never being able to carry a baby. It's being with the man I'm supposed to marry but knowing I'm hurting him by even agreeing to it. *That's* your precious truth, Hugo. You don't get to stand here and say that the truth is the same for me as it is for you. To confess all of this and—what? Expect it to matter? My life has limitations you couldn't possibly know about. You don't get it. You never will."

"Bullshit," Hugo says. And then he reaches forward and pulls me in, puts his arms on my shoulders and holds them there. I can feel the warmth of his palms, the steadfast grip of his fingers. I can feel myself rage up against him. "That's not the truth; that's your story about it. And they aren't the same thing."

My muscles contract. Everything shrinking inward, tighter, closer.

I look at him, defiant. "How the hell would you know?"

"Because," Hugo says. His eyes look into mine—solid black pools. They look like rocks in the water—landing, skipping the surface. "I wrote Jake's note."

Chapter Thirty-Four

Three things happen in rapid succession. The first is that my cell phone rings. The second is that Hugo releases his hold on my shoulders, freeing me to wobble, lose my balance, grab for my phone, and then drop Murphy's leash. The third is that Murphy, now untethered, takes off after the rabbit. I've never seen him run this fast before. He's running like he's just discovered he has legs and wants to test exactly how fast and far they can take him.

"Murphy!"

Before I can even get the word out, Hugo takes off after him. He's a runner, still does six miles every Saturday, but I see him struggle to keep up. Who knew that tiny guy had it in him to be a dog.

I watch them zoom around the reservoir, now blurs in the distance, and I feel an overwhelming sense of helplessness. Because I can't do anything. I am powerless. Murphy could escape, and I can't do anything to stop him.

I walk quickly in their direction, frustrated by my speed—this forced pace. I want to leap. I want to chase after them, screaming at them both. *How could you?*

I wrote Jake's note.

How could that possibly be true? The unthinkable reality of Hugo's interference. What that would make true about my life, my future, this relationship. I focus on Murphy.

When I got back from San Francisco—after my failed relationship with Josh and my failed job—I was devastated. I felt rejected—by Josh, by the professional collapse, by the city itself. For six brief months I had felt connected, engaged—even better than that, *normal.* After, it was like the universe had reminded me—not so fast, Daphne. You're not like the others.

I started apartment hunting in earnest, determined to live on my own even if it meant living in a hovel. I was lucky when I found Gardner Street. The landlord just wanted the right tenant and decided that was me. The first thing I ever brought back to the apartment was Murphy.

"Murphy!"

I'd gone to Petfinder and found a dog at Bark n' Bitches I thought would be mine. I was certain I wanted a Muppet-y dog—curly and happy and bouncy. But when I got there, the dog I was supposed to see was a total dud. They'd named her Daisy, and you could just tell she had no personality. She sat up against the side of her cage and gave me a blank stare—we weren't a match. I started to go, and the woman who ran the place asked if I wanted to see Murphy.

"Murphy!!"

I'd had an imaginary friend when I was younger, exclusively

during my fifth year of life. It was a brief and torrid chapter, but the gentleman who joined my parents and me at dinners and the beach and—much to their chagrin—required his own ticket at the movie theater, was named Murphy. It felt like fate.

Murphy the dog was such a good boy. He didn't bark; he didn't even sniff. They let me foster him for the week, but by the end of the first night I knew he was mine.

"Murphy!!!"

Murphy hates the water but loves to dig at the beach. It's the only place he ever digs. When you give him a haircut he's suddenly so soft it feels like a secret. Like he's been holding all that velvet sweetness right there, right under the surface. He loves sunbeams and gazing out the window. About once a year I cry about the fact that I'll never know what he looked like as a puppy.

The obvious: he's the longest relationship I've ever been in.

"Murphy!" I hear Hugo in the distance.

I keep echoing his calls.

But I can tell it's useless. Murphy is light-years ahead of us now.

I've never even seen him run before. He was the perfect dog for me. He always kept my pace.

Hugo jogs back toward me, his arms at his sides, his palms hanging open, empty.

"I don't know where he went," he says, breathing heavily, his words spaced out and empty. "We should call—"

I keep screaming for him. I clap my hands. "Murphy! Murphy!"

"I'm sorry," he says. "Fuck, Daph, I'm so sorry."

"Murphy!"

"Daphne, listen to me."

"Murphy!"

"I wanted you to know. I—"

I can't lose him. I can't have him disappear from my life. This was my promise, the one living creature I've been able to show up for. I swore I'd keep him safe, I swore I'd never desert him, that I'd tend to him and look after him and in return that he could trust me, that he'd be wise to. He's the only thing that's ever really needed me. The only thing I've ever really done right.

"MURPHY!"

And that's when I see his little body in the distance—just a tiny twirl of white and beige.

"Murphy!"

He runs back at a clip. I see him race into view, coming back to me fast, and I begin to cry. Big tears of relief and love and fury.

He trots up to me. As he gets closer I see that his leash is in his mouth. The first thing I've ever seen him carry there. When he reaches me, he looks up at me, his eyes big and open and wide. And then he drops the leash at my feet.

I'm back. I'm yours.

I bend down and gather him into my arms. I press my face into his fur. I smell the sweet softness of his coat, feel the pulse and rhythm of the blood through his body—this tiny creature. This life. This deep responsibility. "Murphy," I whisper.

I pick up his leash. I wind it around my wrist. I'm still snuggling him close when I look up at Hugo, and on his face I see it—all the anguish I feel. Every impossible question.

"Why?" I ask him.

Hugo's face is red. I don't think I've ever seen him cry before.

Not when I told him I was sick or when we broke up—and not any time since. But his eyes are betraying him now.

"Because," he says. His voice falters. "I wanted you to know what it felt like."

"To what?"

Hugo shakes his head. "To not have a limit."

I stand. I hold Murphy close on the leash. "And you thought it was up to you to decide that? That you should give yourself that kind of power? Hugo, do you have any idea what you've done? I'm marrying him."

"Yeah, and he's perfect for you. And you wouldn't be if you had found that piece of paper."

I stop in my tracks. I feel my blood run cold. Because I hadn't considered that part, hadn't thought about it until right now, right this very instant. "Wait. Was there another note?"

Hugo inhales. I feel his eyes trace my face. "I was in your neighborhood, and I dropped by. I saw it tucked under your door." He pauses, he squints up at the sky. "It said three weeks."

Three weeks. Less than a month. Less than Hugo.

"Jesus, Hugo. Three weeks? He could have been a serial killer!"

"But he wasn't! I knew Kendra was introducing you. And you're not an idiot. You wouldn't have fallen for a serial killer. You wouldn't have committed to him." He blows out an exhale. "Maybe I just wanted you to feel what it felt like to choose."

"Yeah, well, mission accomplished. Feels great right now. Why don't we go try on some wedding dresses!"

I can feel the rage spark through my hands and up through my veins and into my chest. I start walking. Murphy trots beside me, his head forward, as if to say, *I will now behave perfectly in order to make whole my bad behavior.* In other words: *I know what I've done.*

"Where are you going?" Hugo asks.

"Away from here. Right now."

"Daph, please, stop. It doesn't mean anything. You fell in love."

I whirl around. I face him. "Did I?"

I see Hugo's chest rise and not fall. I feel my own breath hover, too.

The moment stretches, then: "No one hates to say this more than me," he says. "But, yeah. You did. And now if you want to be with him it's your decision. Not fate's. Not some piece of paper's. Yours. No one stood a chance, Daph. Not if you couldn't really choose. And now someone does."

I can feel the water rising in my throat. I can feel it sting my eyes. I shut them tight. When I open them, my vision is blurred around the edges.

"I wanted it to be you," I say. Softly, so softly I hope that maybe he cannot even hear me. "I wanted more time."

Hugo's face doesn't change. He keeps his eyes locked on me. "But you got it," he says. He smiles. I see the lines of water down his face like the trails of fingertips. "I'm still here."

Chapter Thirty-Five

When I get home I have no idea what to do. I feel wild, enraged, on fire. I do not know in which direction to burn.

Three weeks.

I think about my third date with Jake, about our first kiss in his apartment, in this apartment, when he cooked me dinner and we gazed out at Los Angeles. Was there an exit point then? Did I just not see one because I wasn't looking? It all felt like open freeway. What would have been our end, otherwise? And then: What would I have made our end?

I sit down on his tan couch. Jake has been wonderful about trying to make this place mine. He's asked me which of my things I might want to take out of storage, if there's any furniture I hate that I'd rather him give away. But I've just said it's fine, I have enough here, which I can tell bothers him a little. I understand it. If this place isn't mine, if I don't make it mine, then it's still only his. Then I don't really live here.

Murphy wanders over to his daybed by the glass doors and plops down into the sunshine. Saber thumps his tail on the couch but stays put. I go into the kitchen and fill a glass with tap water.

Three weeks.

For as long as I can remember I've had an all-or-nothing narrative around love. The movies pitch marriage as some magical undertaking, where you meet a person who is physically molded for you. The feeling of certainty is impenetrable. Everyone is so damn definitive. They know instantly; they say yes without hesitation. But I'd have something better. It wouldn't be a feeling, it would be evidentiary proof.

Even with the air-conditioning the sun is beating through the glass doors. I strip off my T-shirt and leave it tossed down on the counter.

I'm messy, I think. And I hide that from him. Not because I think Jake wouldn't love me but because he deserves better. He deserves better than a woman who leaves her T-shirt on the counter. He deserves someone with baskets and drawers and labels, too. Someone who can adult and understand order. Someone who can provide it.

I peel off my yoga pants next and head into the bathroom. There are mirrors lining the entire wall above the sink, and I catch my reflection. I look brazen, sweaty, wild.

I want to turn away. I normally would. I want to peel off my bra and underwear and get into the shower, let the steam dissolve the mirror, any possible reflection. Fill up this bathroom with liquid smoke.

But instead I stay put, and I stare.

There is a scar down my sternum and two jagged cuts above my left breast. There are bruises there, too, old ones, ones that never heal. They itch; sometimes they burn. These are not dormant things. I lift my fingers to touch my chest, and I coil back. Before my skin can even make contact with its own body, I startle. I've never noticed it before, I've never called it out, but of course it's true. I cannot touch myself where I'm hurt. I cannot lay my own fingers on my skin.

I'm not ready, I think. I am not ready to put my hands on the most vulnerable place, to feel with my own fingers the damage that has been done to me.

So don't touch, I think. *Just look.*

I force myself to meet my own eyes in the mirror. I force myself to see the person across from me. She is wrecked and wretched and distorted. She has been pulled apart. I think about all the times I got dressed hastily, all the times I've worn a turtleneck in the dead of summer, all the times I refused to meet my own body. Every time I turned it over to someone who did not care.

I couldn't look at it because I thought seeing it would mean I'd have to acknowledge the truth: that I was damaged, that I'd never again be organized, tidy—fuck it, *feminine*. But I was wrong. Standing here now I see it. All the glorious reality that makes me who I am. A whole person. A discombobulated whole, a whole that has been stitched and sutured and stapled, but a whole nonetheless.

We have to be cracked open sometimes. We have to be cracked open sometimes to let anything good in. What I see now, emerging in the mirror, is this one, simple truth: learning to be broken is learning to be whole.

I float my hands over my heart. I hover them there. Hummingbirds at the fountain.

"I'm not going anywhere," I say. Out loud. It's a small space and I say it quietly, but I say it. "No matter what, I'm never leaving you."

Chapter Thirty-Six

When I lived with my parents all those years of my extended adolescence, my father and I would have coffee together every morning. He likes to wake up early, just before sunrise, and since I was a light sleeper then, his kitchen rhythms would soon have me out of bed and sitting next to him at the table. We never talked much, just allowed each other to slowly come awake.

"I used to dread the morning because it meant I had to rush out of the house. Then I realized even if I can't make the day longer, I can make the morning earlier," he said.

I never became a morning person. I was only ever awake to see the sunrise during those few hazy years. But now I think maybe I've been missing out. Maybe he's onto something.

I show up at my parents' house the next morning at seven and knock softly at the door. I hear my father's padded footsteps and then there he is—bleary-eyed, his hair standing up every which way, an early-morning Einstein.

"Daphne," he says. "What's wrong?"

A common refrain. But I don't answer. I just start crying. I feel myself exhale and exhale and exhale—everything, all of it. The past five months, the past five years, this decade of being strong and stoic, of never letting myself think or feel the reality of my situation. I exhale the holding back. Of my health, of my heart, of all these paper threads.

"Sweetheart," he says. He puts his arms around me. He holds me close to him. I smell his toothpaste and coffee and yesterday's skin. "Come on in."

I am seated at the counter in my parents' kitchen. My father takes a mug down from the cabinet over the sink and fills it. He dumps in a little creamer—Coffee mate, Irish Crème—and gives it a stir with a spoon. He hands it to me.

"You're sad," he says.

I take a sip. It's hot and sweet. "Captain Obvious." I smile over the rim of my cup. "I don't know," I say. I swallow. Out it comes. "I'm not sure I want to get married."

It's the first time I've said it out loud like this. Maybe it's even the first time I've let myself think it: all the words, right in a row.

My father reacts. I see the surprise on his face, and then the mitigated efforts at resolution. "OK," he says. "What's going on?"

"I'm not sure," I say.

"Oh," he tells me. "I think you are. No one says something like that without a little thought grunt work first. Take me through it."

I put my hands around my mug. I click my nails against the blue ceramic. My parents bought these mugs on a trip to Seattle.

I know because in the past ten years, it's the only vacation they ever took.

You're not the only one who has sacrificed, I think.

"You know, when I got sick it made sense to me, in a strange way. It's like there was always something different about me, like I behaved different, my life was different. I thought I deserved it. But now—I don't want to punish myself anymore."

My father nods. It's cool in the kitchen, and he still wears his robe over his pajamas. It's a blue paisley terry cloth. My mother ordered a striped one from a catalog and they sent this floral one instead. "Why can't I wear it?" I remember my father asking. "I like flowers, too."

"What changed?"

"Time?" I say, although I think maybe it's more than that. Maybe it's something else, some other unseeable force.

"Jake is a nice guy," my father says. "We'd be happy to have him as a part of our family."

I feel my stomach clench, and I brace myself. I know, after all, how my father surely wants someone to be here to take care of me when he isn't. Who could blame him? Hell, I should get married for that reason alone.

"I know," I say. "He's kind and considerate, and he always leaves the toilet seat down. He's honestly perfect."

My father takes a sip of coffee and then looks back up at me. "He is," he says. "But that doesn't matter much if he isn't perfect for you."

I think about Jake proposing at Moonshadows, all the hope in his heart—all the hope he *presented* to me. I took it. I wanted to. But this hope feels heavy, too heavy to hold. I want lightness.

"He's willing to sign up for all of this," I say. "And it's not fair."

My father's voice is gentle. "What, exactly?"

I feel my throat constrict. I don't like to talk about my heart with my father. Not because it's painful for me but because it is for him. I don't like to remind him what isn't fair to him, either. But I put that aside now. Because I need to say it. "That I'll leave him. That I'm forcing him to sign up for this at all. That I can't promise him another day."

I see the gravity of this settle on my father. He sets his mug down. He comes around the counter and puts his hands on my shoulders. I look into his warm, brown, caring eyes. I see so much there—the wrinkles around his forehead, the gray hair at his temples. All the signs of someone growing old, the way the thickness of life recedes and recedes until it's translucent.

"Chicken," he says. The lines around his mouth wobble. I can see how much effort it is taking to say what he does next. "I think about you all the time. Most of the moments of my day, in fact. Even when I'm doing something, at the market or on a run, I'm thinking about you. I'm thinking about how much I want you to be well. I'd give anything to fix it so that you could be. I pray for it every night. I have for thirteen years. If you knew the bargains I have tried to make with the universe—" His voice breaks and his eyes fill up. He shakes his head. "There isn't a day that goes by that I do not wish it was me. Hell, they made a mistake, Daphne. It should have been."

"Dad—"

"That's what we do for our children. We wish it were us."

I feel the warmth of his strong and steady palms.

"But the thing is, Daphne. No one's time is promised. Not

yours. Not Mom's. Not mine. Not Jake's. It's just the way it is. We are all dying. Every day. And at some point it becomes a choice. Which one are you going to do today? Are you living or are you dying?"

My father looks right at me. His face is soft. He looks at me in a way I can only describe as open. I think, perhaps, this is the first time I have ever, in more than thirteen years, invited him to show me his grief.

"And, honey," he says. "All I wish for you, for any of us, is to do the living one. To do it to the fullest. For as long as it lasts."

Tears spill down his face. I've only ever witnessed my dad cry once, all those years ago, in a quiet corner of a hospital room.

My mother was asleep in a chair. They were running so many tests in those early days, and I was exhausted all the time. It felt like I was in a perpetual haze.

I awoke, but my eyes were still closed, and I heard my father next to me. No, I felt him. I felt his hand in mine, sitting right next to my hospital bed, and then his lips on my fingers and then the wet of his tears. I kept my eyes closed as he wept into my palm.

"Please," I remember him whispering. Just the one word. *Please.*

"My child, my baby girl."

I could feel the well of his grief, and I remember thinking I never wanted to see this much vulnerability from anyone ever again. I remember thinking: *This is terrifying.*

Looking at my father before me now, I realize how much I've been denying the people who love me. I didn't want them to know I was in pain or short of breath. I didn't want them to know the new drugs made me feel tired or heavy or anxious. I didn't want them to know I thought about it—how much time I have left. I didn't want my sickness reflected on their faces. But more than that, I didn't want to see their own weakness. I didn't want to feel their tender and heartbroken humanity. Because then it would confirm it all, everything I feared. That it was just as serious as I suspected. That I was in that much trouble.

It's not bad, I think, as I watch my father cry now. *It hurts and it's painful, but it's not bad.* Pain and bad are not the same thing.

I thought if I had all the answers, if I was always one step ahead, if I knew my hand, then I'd never lose. But being surprised by life isn't losing, it's living. It's messy and uncomfortable and complicated and beautiful. It's life, all of it. The only way to get it wrong is to refuse to play.

I look at my father, and I see the man I saw in the hospital room all those years ago—broken and open. But where there was once helplessness there is now something else. These are not the tears of desperation but rather acknowledgment—of all we have accepted. Of everything we still do not know.

"He wants to protect me," I say. "Jake does. But he can't."

My father laughs. It is a gentle laugh. A skip of a laugh. A little hop over sorrow. "Your mother started saying something to me right after my father died, and she kept telling me in those years after your diagnosis, too, when, damn, I needed to hear it." He exhales. "Love is a net."

He looks right at me. His eyes are gentle. I see in them the enormity of his grief, the enormity of his love.

"She would tell me all the time that the love we had mattered, that it could catch you, that it *was* catching you." He shakes his head. I see his mouth move, uneven, overcome. "So, no, he cannot give you forty more years, but, baby, love is the most powerful force we've got. If you think protection isn't in its jurisdiction, you're wrong."

I sit back. I suck in a breath.

"I don't know what to do," I tell him.

"Sweetheart," he says. He squeezes my hand. His grip is strong, assured. "Sure you do." He smiles at me. There is a glint in his eye. "You just do what's in your heart."

Chapter Thirty-Seven

I meet Jake at the parking lot on Ocean Avenue that's a short walk to Santa Monica Beach. He arrives in the old, beat-up Chevy.

"No breakdowns on the Ten," he says. "New record. I still have no idea why I take this thing anywhere."

He's wearing khaki shorts and a blue long-sleeved T-shirt. His hair looks red in the sunlight.

"Why do you, anyway?" I ask. I shove my hands down into the pockets of my jean shorts. I can feel them vibrating.

He looks at his car—a heaping pile of rubbish, really—and then back to me. But I realize I already know as soon as I say it.

"She gave it to me for my twenty-second birthday," he says. "It was always a lemon. But I love the damn thing. I like to drive it fast, with the top down, which is a douche move. But it feels alive to me, you know?"

I nod.

"Should we walk?" I ask.

He takes my hand, and we cross the street and walk down the wire-gated pathway to the ocean. It's almost six and the sun is still overhead, the whole beach bathed in light.

"I think four thirty will be perfect," he says when we're down there. "It'll give us at least an hour, even in the fall."

Fifty paces down, the ocean yawns and exhales. There are no waves along this stretch of beach really. It's made for toddlers and paddleboarders.

The sand underneath us is wet and heavy, and when my feet sink down, I wiggle my toes, letting it fold in between them.

I once read that there are more stars in the sky than there are grains of sand on earth. It seemed impossible. It always seems impossible to believe the things we cannot see.

"Jake," I say. I squeeze his palm.

The thing I remember from the night I met Jake is that I was in a hurry. I'd just come home from work fifteen minutes before I was meant to leave. I didn't have time to take a shower, I didn't even have time to be too intentional about my outfit. I didn't necessarily want to go. There is something that happens when you've been single too long—you decide what things will be before you experience them. I figured Jake was a nice guy. That we'd have minimal chemistry. That the whole thing would be a night I could have spent on my couch with Murphy.

And then I got the note. What is that saying? "Man's greatest fear is not that he is inadequate but that he is powerful beyond measure?" Something like that. I never really understood it, but I do now. Because power is responsibility.

All my life I had been waiting for the note that would tell

me it was finally time to stand still. That the long, broken road was over. That *he* was finally here. But when it came, all I felt was fear. Fear that he wouldn't be who I'd imagined. Fear that I wasn't ready. Fear that I wouldn't feel the way I was supposed to. Fear that I'd fuck up even this, this thing I was meant for. But what I was most afraid of, maybe, was that it was over. It's hard to be single, but it's also something you can get good at. And I was good at it.

It's easy to love the things we are good at.

"Yes?" Jake threads his fingers through my own.

Yes, I wanted epic love. Weak-in-the-knees, movie-kiss-in-the-rain epic love. What I never realized, not up until this very moment, is that I got it—everything I'd been asking for. I'd been on the back of a motorcycle in Paris and across the Golden Gate Bridge at sunrise. I'd been on the beach in Santa Monica at sunset. My life has been filled with magical moments, I was just so busy waiting I didn't see them when they were here.

Density, I think. I try to hold on to this moment. I try to fall to the depths of it. And it's there, in the reflections in the water at the very bottom, that I know what I need to do next.

It's easy to pretend you do not know while you're waiting, but it's impossible once the truth arrives.

"I can't marry you," I say. I see myself at the surface—coughing, sputtering—new life in my lungs.

Jake turns to look at me. His hand is still in mine.

"Daphne."

"I know," I say. "Believe me, I know. I've done a lot of bad things in my life, but this takes the cake. And it's idiotic, to boot. You're the one. You're so clearly the one."

I think about Jake in the mornings, bringing me an espresso and a water with fresh lemon juice. I think about him cooking for us in the kitchen at night. I think about the way he knows how to fix a leaky faucet and how he now lays my medicine out for me, every day, in a smiley face on a bright yellow plate. As if to say, *Let's be happy in this.* As if to say, *Only good things here.*

"I've been looking for you for a very long time," I say. "And when I found you I just felt so lucky to have you that I didn't realize I had it wrong."

"You had what wrong?" He shakes his head. "Is this about the baby thing? It's fine. We don't have to do it. I just wanted to talk—"

"No," I say. "And yes. You want kids. That's OK. You should have the things you want, Jake."

"I never said that. You're twisting my words. I was trying to have an open conversation with you. If you're getting married, it's natural to talk about—"

"But I don't know if it's what I want. I don't know if I can. And I want to accept that, but you don't have to." I look at him. I see the pain in his face.

Pain is not bad.

"You couldn't save her, Jake. And I'm sorry for that. I'm sorry for you. But you can't make up for it by trying to save me."

Jake runs a hand down his face. "That is a really shitty thing to say to me," he says.

"Yes. But I'm not wrong."

I feel us both give to the weight of the moment. Everything settles into the sand. And then, all at once, I have the intense instinct to change my mind. To take it all back. I'll never be with someone this perfect for me. I'll never find someone this understanding. I'm ruining it. I'm ruining it because I do not yet know how to hold it and hold myself at the same time.

"For the first time in my life I've been honest with the people around me about who I am," I say. "I don't know what it's like to live and not apologize to myself, or for myself. I need to find out."

Jake nods.

"This does not feel real," he says.

"I know."

He drags a foot back and forth, making tracks in the sand.

"So now what?" he says.

I used to think the unknown was impossible—that all it brought was pain and fear and a red-blinking clock, counting down the minutes. Now I know that's not true, at least, it's not the only thing that is true. The unknown can be beautiful. A surprise can be flowers on your doorstep. It can be a piece of paper that ends up changing your life.

What is blank space, really, but an invitation?

Jake pinches the bridge of his nose with his thumb and forefinger. He squints his eyes closed. I see it all there—the hurt and disbelief. Of ending up here. Of starting over.

"You deserve something easy and joyful and uncomplicated," I tell him.

He looks at me. I see the green in his eyes, reflecting off the water. "But I don't want that," he says. "I want you."

We are powerful because we affect each other's stories, all of us. We are here to impact each other, to knock into each other, to throw each other off-balance, sometimes even off track. I've always hated the phrase "There's a reason for everything." As if my illness were built into my story; as if it were inevitable; as if it were a good thing and not something I would blink away in an instant if I could. But here, now, I think even if there's not a reason for everything, there may be a reason for everyone.

"You do want that," I say. "You just don't know it yet. You've been used to hard for such a long time."

Jake stuffs his hands into his pockets. The sun is setting now. The oranges and pinks give way to cool blues. And at the end of a warm day it's still breezy at the beach. In another twenty minutes, we'll need sweaters.

And that's when a group of teenagers walk by. They're wearing low-slung jeans and hooded sweatshirts, and every last one of them is carrying a pair of Doc Martens black boots, laces tied, slung like ice skates over their shoulders.

My eyes widen. I look to Jake. He sees, too, reaches into his back pocket and takes out his notebook and a pen. He looks incredulous. He writes something down.

I study him. As he's scrawling I see his Adam's apple move.

"What is this about?" I say. "Really."

He caps his pen and deposits both back into his pocket. When he looks up, his eyes are red.

"Of course," I say.

A wink. A smile. *I'm watching you*, or *Everything is going to be all right.*

Love is a net. It can catch you long after the person is no longer there.

"When you are ready," Jake says, his eyes on the sea, "someone is going to be very lucky."

I feel the ocean exhale. Relief at relinquishing to its shores what it can no longer hold.

"We'll see," I tell him.

He nods. "We'll see."

Chapter Thirty-Eight

Kendra and I are having a cup of tea on Irina's deck. Inside, Irina pours herself a glass of wine. I see her open the refrigerator, take out a bowl of berries, and walk outside to join us. Her backyard is all stone—slate floors, built-in rock benches, and a wall of greenery behind us. There's a firepit in the center, although it's warm enough now to not need it. Her backyard is my favorite oasis. An unholy marriage of spa, redwood forest, and English garden.

"Gooseberries," she says. She sets down a bowl of raspberries and round, golden fruit. "Low glycemic index and excellent for your liver." She smiles at us.

I pop one in my mouth. It's tart and sweet. Almost the consistency of a sour grape but juicier.

"These are good," I say.

Kendra tries one. "Strange."

"Strange and good is my favorite combo," Irina says. She sits down next to us on the custom pillow-clad stone bench and crosses her legs. She's wearing jeans and a sweater—a rare casual sight. "So, how are you?"

They both turn to look at me. We are here, in Irina's backyard, because I am newly single again. Or rather, the intention of this night is to both buoy and unpack that reality.

"Fine," I say. "I got my last box on Wednesday."

My old apartment was already rented, but as it turned out my landlord, Mike, had another property down the block. It's not as big as my last place, but it's newly updated, fresh paint on the walls, and with about a quarter of my stuff in it, it looks almost spacious.

"How was it?" Irina asks.

"He hates me."

"Please. He doesn't hate you," Kendra says. "He loves you. It's hard to love someone and not be with them."

I take a sip of tea—spearmint.

"It doesn't feel like love right now," I say.

When I went to pick up my last box, Jake wasn't there. All that was left was a note: "Your sneakers are in the hall closet."

That's it. He hadn't even taken them out. But who could blame him.

"Oh, how the hell do you know," Irina says. "You're an infant."

"Not quite," I say.

She waves me off. "You know love isn't enough—I've said it to you before—but that's basic shit. Everyone knows that. You need water and food and toilet paper, to start. Obviously. The thing no one talks about is what love actually *is*." Irina uncrosses her legs and leans forward, elbows on knees. "Penelope and I have been through nearly every iteration of this dance you can do. We've been committed and married and separated and friends. We've had every different kind of love they talk about, at a hundred different points. The key to love is this, baby: Can you move together?"

Kendra starts laughing. I turn to her next to me. "What?"

"I'm just remembering your first wedding," she tells Irina. "You brought out that boa constrictor that everyone thought was real."

"He was real," Irina says, somewhat wearily. "He was sleeping."

"She's right," Kendra says. "Joel and I don't work because he's my person, we work because I feel like I can be every bad and impossible version of myself with him. I can change. And it's not even that I know he'll still love me, it's that it's not even a question, he has."

"I just have no idea what comes next."

Kendra puts her arm around me. Irina picks up her wineglass.

"Next we go to Italy," Irina says.

"Italy?"

I look from Irina to Kendra, who shrugs.

"I'm producing the new Oceans. You may have heard? And I'd like you to come with me. But not as my assistant," Irina says. "As a producer."

My mouth drops open. I can physically feel my jaw unhinge.

"What? You don't think that's what you've been doing? You do notes, you handle schedules, you made a budget for our last feature. Listen, no one would like you to stay my assistant forever more than me, but it's time to look toward the future, Daphne. You're already producing. We're just going to make it official now."

"I—"

"I've never had anyone work for me who was as determined and resourceful and who this came so easily to—" Irina looks to Kendra. "Honestly, you should take some offense to all of this."

Kendra laughs. "I do."

Irina turns her attention back to me. I look at her face. Her raised eyebrows, her bright red lipstick. There is a smile playing on her lips.

"So, what do you say?" she asks.

It's the easiest yes I've ever given.

Chapter Thirty-Nine

Daphne, sixteen months later.

I'm balancing a shopping bag, a purse, and an iced tea when my cell phone rings. Hugo is calling.

"Hi," I say. "Hi! I am about to drop a very cold and very large beverage."

"Lovely visual. Where are you?"

"On Little Santa Monica."

I'm headed toward the Le Pain Quotidien between Camden and Bedford in Beverly Hills. The wind is riled here, but then it always is in the fall. The Santa Anas land, and they stir everything up. Dust, dirt, skirts, last season's grievances. They're all up for grabs.

"I thought you had a hot date."

I smile. I shift my bag up onto my shoulder. "We've been over this," I say. "It's not a date. It's just coffee."

"Does he know that?"

"He does," I say.

"You better hurry. If you're late he might get the message you're not interested at all."

"Hugo!" I say. "It's not even two thirty yet. And this phone call isn't helping. I'm hanging up now."

I am in need of caffeine today—hence the iced tea—but now I just feel jittery. All the bubbles in my stomach jiggle and begin to pop. During our five-month stint in Rome I picked up a bad espresso habit I'm having a hard time shaking.

"Not yet," he says. "I have more things to say."

I'm standing on the corner of Camden. I look down the block at the restaurant on the left-hand side. I think about what is waiting for me in there.

Time is a funny thing. The way it doubles back and leaps forward. The way six years can pass in a blink but a moment can stretch to a decade.

"OK," I say. "But fair warning. I'm almost there."

I start walking. And then I'm outside the door to the restaurant. There are some tables out front, on the sidewalk. A couple in their sixties shares a sandwich, two teen girls bend their heads over iced coffees.

I look in, through the glass, and there he is. He's gesturing to the waiter—laughing. I see the relaxed bend of his legs, the friendly gesturing of his arms. I am all at once bowled over by the reality that there are still new stories to tell. That not everything is known or explored. That there are great and wondrous things ahead. That nothing is promised and yet, and yet . . .

I am about to walk inside when I feel a tap on my shoulder.

"Excuse me, Miss?"

I turn around and see a woman. She's in her mid-fifties, wearing a blue button-down and a pair of wide-legged black pants.

"I think you dropped this?"

She holds out a piece of paper to me. No bigger than a postcard. I think about the box under my bed. I still have it. All those sheets of paper. They are photographs, now, snapshots of a past. They each tell a story, one I am grateful for. *Without you*, I think. *Without you I would not have everything that came next.*

The woman holds the paper out to me. Right there, right between her fingers. And as she looks at me expectantly I begin to laugh.

She is confused, at first—how odd! A funny piece of paper? But then she joins in.

Joy is contagious, I think.

I take it, and she leaves, waving over her shoulder as she goes.

"Have a great day!" she calls to me.

It could be a fallen bill or a hastily written-down number—some other explicable thing from the depths of my bag. But it could also not be.

"What's going on?" Hugo asks through the phone.

I don't answer.

I hold it between my fingers—this promise, this premonition—and just as I'm about to open it the wind picks up. It plucks the paper straight out of my hands. It carries it—down the block and into the street, where it mingles with other lost items—receipts and wrappers, envelopes and candy, the forgotten cigarette, the apple core.

I consider grabbing for it—chasing it down. I could catch it, maybe, if I moved fast, if I moved *now*. But then it's too late—the moment passes me by, and it's indistinguishable from everything surrounding it.

I look at the swirl of dust and paper and dirt—people cover their faces. One woman struggles by with an umbrella.

"Ay!" she says. "This weather!"

I smile into the street.

Goodbye, I think, although that is not the right word. What I mean is something else, something that is not possible to convey in a singular expression. Something that is not at all an ending.

And then I turn back toward the door, and walk inside.

I hear Hugo's voice through the phone. Calm and steady and familiar. "You look beautiful," he says.

I hadn't realized I was still holding it. And then he gets up from his seat by the window and walks over to me. He takes the phone off my ear and out of my hand.

"Hi," he says.

"Hi."

We stand that way, grinning at each other, until a waitress comes over. We are in the way, could we please take a seat? Hugo holds his arm out and gestures toward his table—toward his half-drunk coffee and the leather jacket looped over the back of his chair. I think about our first meeting, in that parking lot all those years ago. How much has changed, and changed again. I could never have seen this. I have no idea what happens now.

"Here we are," he says, somewhat nervously, somewhat, even, earnestly.

Here we are.

Acknowledgments

To my agent, Erin Malone, without whom I'd have none of this. We surpassed wildest dreams a long time ago and we're still going. I love everything about doing this with you.

To my editor, Lindsay Sagnette, the greatest partner and teammate. Thank you for your blind and unyielding faith in me, my words, and my future.

To my publisher, Libby McGuire, who is simply the best in the business.

To Jon Karp for continuing to make Simon & Schuster such a wonderful home.

To my manager, David Stone, who guides my career with the utmost intelligence, grace, and humility.

To Dana Trocker, for the cold hard facts.

To Ariele Fredman, still, and to Falon Kirby—thank you.

To Jade Hui, Alexandra Figueroa, Caitlin Mahony, Matilda

Forbes Watson, and Alicia Everett for their support, time, enthusiasm, and compassion.

To Hilary Zaitz Michael and Chelsea Radler for believing these stories deserve to be told in other mediums.

To everyone at WME and Simon & Schuster who work so incredibly hard on behalf of me and my novels. My gratitude is endless.

To Leilani Graham for your keen eye and deep generosity.

To the Wednesday Crew plus Murphy. I cherish our community. Five stars.

To my parents, who are such great gifts in my life.

And to you. I was single for a very long time. When I sat down to write this book, I told my editor: "I want to write about the search for love, and I think if I write it honest, he'll be there at the end of it." When I finished it, I wrote her: "You know how I write a note at the end of all my books to my readers? This time the note is the novel." Everything I'd like to say about that incredibly winding journey is in these pages. All of Daphne's chapters matter, just like all of mine did, just like all of yours do.

Incidentally, he was there at the end of it, but that's a story for another time . . .

BONUS CONTENT

A Coffee Shop, Some Shoes, and a Love Story Worth Waiting For

They met in college but reconnected sixteen years later. Romance blossomed.

Jake Green, 37, and Elana Barr first crossed paths back in 2008 when they attended the University of Portland. "She worked at the local coffee shop," said Mr. Green. "She was the barista you wanted because she'd always give the students an extra shot of espresso. I must have been in there every day." He remembers one particular Sunday during a very heavy rainstorm. "It was pouring outside and I, stupidly, was wearing flip-flops. My feet were soaked, and I had to bike home." He recalls Ms. Barr's compassion. "She offered me a pair of Doc Martens," he says. "They weren't hers, they were in the back office, but I took them and weirdly they fit. I never forgot it."

Ms. Barr, 37, who is keeping her name, remembers things a little differently. "What?!" she says, laughing. "Why would I give away someone else's shoes?"

After graduation, Ms. Barr went on to be a successful children's book illustrator, bringing to life family favorites such as *Outside Here* and *The New York Times* bestselling series *The Pineapple and P.*

Mr. Green began working in entertainment and married his college sweetheart, Beatrice Fanelli. They were just twenty-seven when she passed away of a rare type of breast cancer. "It was the most devastating time in my life," says Mr. Green. "But it changed things for me. I understood how fragile life is, and how necessary love is." When asked if he knew he'd marry again, Mr. Green says unequivocally yes. "I wanted to put all that love to good use."

Ms. Barr put roots down in Portland while Mr. Green's life eventually took him to Los Angeles. He was home last summer after a particularly bad breakup when he encountered Ms. Barr again. It had been sixteen years since the coffee shop, and the shoes.

"I went to a reading at Powell's. I really just needed to get out of the house. It ended up being storybook hour there. They were reading Elana's latest book."

"It was him and a bunch of four-year-olds," Ms. Barr says. "He was hard to miss."

"She was so charismatic up there," says the groom, beaming. "I immediately felt like I'd known her before."

Mr. Green bought a book, which Ms. Barr very graciously signed. He asked her if she'd like to have coffee, and she accepted. It was not until they were seated that they realized they'd both attended the university at the same time. The bride told the groom about her prior job while a student there. "And then I put two and two together," Mr. Green says. "I told her about the shoes."

She didn't remember, but she did gesture down to her feet. Sure enough, she was wearing a pair of Doc Martens.

"I don't even know why," Ms. Barr says. "They aren't really my style and I'd never worn them before. But it was raining that day."

Mr. Green says that was the moment he knew. "It was the shoes for me," he says. "And her smile. It lit up the biggest bookstore in the world."

Mr. Green moved back to Portland just four months later and the two got engaged three months after that.

They were cooking dinner in the couple's flat in the Pearl District in March when Mr. Green got down on one knee and presented Ms. Barr with an opal, a family heirloom.

"I was roasting a chicken with juice on my hands and the next thing I know, Barry Manilow starts playing. Jake told me that all he ever wanted was this night, on repeat, forever. I of course said yes."

The couple were married at the groom's family's home in Portland last Saturday, August 23. The bride wore a garland of dried pink roses and eucalyptus in her hair, and the couple's dog, Saber, carried the rings in his collar down the aisle.

"She's made me feel more at home than I ever have before," Mr. Green says. "With her, it's just easy."

Daphne's Seventy-Two Hours in Los Angeles

FRIDAY

9:00 a.m.: You wake up jet-lagged, maybe—time to grab some coffee at Kings Road Cafe. Get an iced Americano with some oat milk. It'll keep you going for hours, plus 2% cow's milk is essentially illegal in Los Angeles. Grab a muffin while you're there, or a juice across the street at Beverly Hills Juice. The Green Genie is a go-to.

Next up is a hike at Bronson Canyon. It's the best view of the Hollywood sign, but only if you make it up to the top. Five miles round trip. Or, if you're me, you walk around the entryway to the park. Turn right when the path leads straight, and you'll end up at the base of some incredible jagged rocks. Then turn around. There's an excellent view there, too, and you didn't even have to climb.

Shower, change. (This is important.) I can't give hotel recommendations because everywhere you stay in Los Angeles is overpriced and the places that are truly worth it cost the equivalent of a down payment on a small home. Good luck!

1:00 p.m.: Lunch is at Erewhon in Beverly Hills on Beverly. Grab a wrap or a sushi roll, and a Hailey Bieber smoothie if you must, and sit outside and people-watch.

Spend the afternoon browsing the stores on Rodeo Drive. It's touristy, but you can't come to LA and not do a little 90210 damage.

7:00 p.m.: Finish Friday with dinner at Shu at the Glen Centre—a hidden gem in the hills of Bel Air. A guy I dated once told me he thought it would be the perfect place to bring someone you were having an affair with.

SATURDAY

Wake up late, order room service coffee, and then make your way over to Palisades Village. It's a little like Pleasantville, but hey, this is LA.

12:30 p.m.: Have lunch at The Draycott—make sure to get the English pea dip—and browse around.

7:30 p.m.: Dinner is at Tower Bar. It's a scene, so come prepared. Get the burger, maybe a martini. The make-your-own sundae complete with pen and paper is a must. Dress the part.

If you're feeling up for it, go get some laughs at The Comedy Store late night. Look out for Iliza Shlesinger working out new material.

SUNDAY

10:00 a.m.: Coffee at Alfred on Melrose Place to cure what ails you. A chagaccino will likely not go down well after three martinis, but try.

Spend whatever you have left of the day browsing Melrose Avenue. Hit up Ron Herman, Melrose Trading Post, and Wasteland.

5:00 p.m.: Dinner is at Hotel Bel Air. It's pricey, but worth it. Get there early and grab an outdoor couch in their bar area. Order cocktails and ask for bar snacks.

Then it's on to dinner. There is no off-menu pomodoro, but you can ask. Tell them I sent you.

Expiration Dates

Rebecca Serle

This reading group guide for Expiration Dates *includes discussion questions, ideas for enhancing your book club, and a Q&A with author Rebecca Serle. The suggested questions are intended to help your reading group find new and interesting angles and topics for your discussion. We hope that these ideas will enrich your conversation and increase your enjoyment of the book.*

Topics & Questions for Discussion

1. When we first learn about Daphne's slips of paper, she says, "Something else has always called the shots in my life—call it the universe, fate, the comedic force of timing." How does this set up the conversation about destiny versus choice throughout the novel?

2. In chapter 4, Daphne says, "But I still wanted forever love. I still wanted my perfect mate, my smiling husband. I'd picture the white tulle dress and the lace veil and a man who was kind and attractive and who my parents loved, because why not." How is Daphne's description of her perfect man different at the end of the novel?

3. How does the Daphne who dates Jake differ from the versions of her with previous men? How does she change over the course of their relationship and for what reasons?

4. Hugo is one of the most important people in Daphne's life. How does their relationship alter over the course of the

novel, and how does Hugo contribute to Daphne's understanding of happiness for herself?

5. When Jake asks Daphne to move in with him, what does Daphne's reaction tell us about what this next step in the relationship means for her? What are the factors that make her want to say yes or say no?

6. There's a major twist in the novel regarding Daphne's health. Why do you think the author decided to introduce the twist where she did, and how does it contribute to the larger message of the novel?

7. Why do you think Daphne felt she had to keep her health condition and her slips of paper a secret? Why does she ultimately decide to divulge that information?

8. In chapter 25, after Hugo, Jake, and Daphne have dinner together, Jake says, "I feel for him, Daphne. . . . It's not his fault he's still in love with you." What was your reaction to that scene?

9. Similarly to Daphne, Jake brings his own history and baggage into their relationship. How does Jake's past affect his relationship with Daphne?

10. We discover toward the end of the novel that Hugo wrote Jake's note, starting Daphne and Jake's relationship. Why do you think Hugo did what he did, and how does it speak to

the core question of destiny versus choice at the heart of the novel?

11. Sense of environment is a major theme in many Rebecca Serle novels, and this time she set the novel in Los Angeles. What parts of LA came alive for you, and how was the story enriched by this setting?

12. Were you surprised that Jake and Daphne did not end up together? What do you think this means for Daphne's journey and her resolution at the end of the book?

13. One of the last lines of the novel reads, "*Goodbye*, I think, although that is not the right word. What I mean is something else, something that is not possible to convey in a singular expression. Something that is not at all an ending." What do you think Daphne means by this?

Enhance Your Book Club

1. Discuss how you came to find love in your life, how it relates to or differs from Daphne's experience, and how the journey to find love looks different for everyone.

2. Read *In Five Years* and *One Italian Summer*, and discuss how Rebecca uses magical realism and themes of love (in all forms) in each of her novels.

3. Visit rebeccaserle.com to learn more about the author and the inspiration behind this book.

A Conversation with Rebecca Serle

Q: There is a magical realism element to all of your books, with Daphne's slips of paper in *Expiration Dates*, but also in *One Italian Summer* and *In Five Years*. How does magic allow you to explore your characters and the larger themes you discuss in your books?

A: Magic is a way into the books that can just cut to the heart of what I'm trying to say faster. You could tell Daphne's story as someone who is a serial dater and who is trying to kind of game the system, game life, but why not just give her a little bit of magic? I like that my protagonists have something other people don't. It allows me to really look at what makes them special.

Q: Daphne dates a revolving door of men throughout the novel, and each has their own distinct personality. How were you able to instill each character with their own deep history? Where did you draw your inspiration from?

A: Listen, I met my husband when I was almost thirty-seven . . . I come by that revolving door honestly! I know what it feels like to search, and some of the experiences that come along with that, but no one in the book IS anyone I was ever with. They are all facets of Daphne's journey, and what she needs to learn. Some of our lessons were similar, but a lot of them were not. The men all give her something, so it was easy to figure out who they were when I let Daphne lead.

Q: There are beautiful descriptions of Los Angeles throughout the novel. Is there a reason why you chose to set the novel in LA?
A: Los Angeles is my home now, just like New York was my home for many years. I love LA—and not the LA that people think about when they think about "Hollywood." Daphne's Los Angeles has a lot of overlap with mine, and I had a lot of fun writing it.

Q: Daphne has a beautiful, endearing relationship with her parents. Why is this dynamic important to her character and the message of the novel as a whole?
A: Well, I mean, the relationships between adult children and their parents are clearly something I like to talk about! I love my parents and I am very aware, as well, of what it means to grow up—how a certain part of us has to leave them behind, in a sense. Daphne relies on her parents in ways maybe other thirtysomethings don't. And there's beauty and pain in that. We want our parents to protect us always—but of course, they can't protect us from life, not really. Part of growing up is realizing that. But also—and this is a line in the book—realizing that "love is a net." So even if they can't save us, exactly, their love endures.

Q: We see Daphne at different points in her life over the course of the novel. Why did you feel it was important to show the

reader who Daphne was when she was coming of age, who she is in the present, and who she becomes months after the ultimate resolution?
A: I wanted these slips of paper to be something she's lived with forever; they've been with her for a very long time. And when it comes to the search for love—listen, it looks different in your twenties than in your thirties. I wanted to represent all of that.

Q: Why is Daphne's heart condition important to her character? How did you hope it would speak to the message of the book?
A: I knew I wanted to write about the search for love, and then when I came up with this idea—a woman receives slips of paper that tell her how long her relationships will last—it felt exciting, but a little bit trite. I couldn't figure out WHY this was her story. When I realized she had a heart condition, everything made sense. None of our time is promised, right? It's the one thing we know for sure: not one of us gets out of here alive. Yet we spend our whole lives trying to run from that one, singular truth. Daphne is no different.

Q: I think we can all agree that Murphy is the cutest dog with the most personality. Why did you decide to include him in the novel?
A: My dear friend Morgan Matson has a dog named Murphy who shares every single thing in common with Murphy in the book, including his love/fear of bunnies and his big, beautiful heart and dapper personality. Thank you for letting me borrow him, Morgan!

Q: You found true love while writing this novel. Can you speak to that experience, how it contributed to the novel, and vice versa?

A: I met my husband three months after I finished the first draft. I will say that my love story, when it arrived, felt less like the ending to my single years and more like the start of something else entirely. It's a different conversation. *Expiration Dates* is really about the search. Finding and holding love is a different book.

Q: Can you tell us anything about your next book?

A: I would imagine that book will take us deeper into commitment—both in family and in love. We shall see!

About the Author

Rebecca Serle is the *New York Times* bestselling author of *One Italian Summer*, *In Five Years*, *The Dinner List*, and the young adult novels *The Edge of Falling* and *When You Were Mine*. Serle also developed the hit TV adaptation *Famous in Love,* based on her YA series of the same name. She is a graduate of USC and the New School and lives in Los Angeles with her husband and daughter. Find out more at RebeccaSerle.com.